COLLECTORS

COLLECTORS

A NOVEL

PAUL GRINER

RANDOM HOUSE

NEW YORK

Library of Congress Cataloging-in-Publication Data

Griner, Paul.
Collectors / Paul Griner.
p.   cm.
ISBN 0-679-44846-2
I. Title.
PS3557.R5314C65   1999
813'.54—dc21   99-14153

website address: www.atrandom.com

Printed in the United States of America on acid-free paper

2 4 6 8 9 7 5 3

First Edition

Book design by Fritz Metsch

FOR MY PARENTS

AND

FOR NICOLE ARAGI

ACKNOWLEDGMENTS

Special thanks to those who have read and generously commented on the material in this book at various stages: Laura Griner, Chris Kennedy, Lynne McFall, Jeff Skinner, and Toby Wolff. To my editor, Dan Menaker, my heartfelt thanks for pushing for a better book. Jeanne Tift and Jean-Isabel McNutt made some excellent suggestions, and I thank them along with the rest of the staff at Random House for making the editing process so pleasurable.

I am always and very much indebted to my agent, Nicole Aragi, for her unwavering support, friendship, and fine judgment. Thanks, too, to the staff at Watkins/Loomis.

Finally, greatest thanks of all to my wife, Anne. Without her, this book would not exist.

COLLECTORS

THE CHURCH BELLS STRUCK THREE FOR THE HOUR, THEN began ringing in celebration, so loudly that at first it was impossible to talk, and outside the church it was hot and windy. Dust blew down the street and over all their heads, the women's dresses clung to their bodies, Claudia's veil was billowing. It whipped in her face, distracting her, and then her cousin Jean appeared in the line, looking collected and cool despite the wind and the midday heat, wearing a sleeveless mint-green dress and heels. Under her arm was an elegant bag. Claudia clasped her to herself briefly, intrigued but not surprised to detect the scent of *Fracas*—her own perfume—and then passed Jean on to Boyd, her new husband.

"And this is my cousin Jean," she said, her hand on Jean's bare shoulder.

Boyd had been talking to the blond in front of Jean, flirting really, and now he turned to Jean and tilted his large head to the side. "Sorry," he said. "I didn't catch your name." Smiling, he took Jean's offered hand in both of his.

He was beefy and broad, but his touch lacked force, and even at his full height, Jean guessed, he wouldn't be as tall as she. She straightened and felt Claudia's fingers leaving her skin one after the other, like a string of pearls being plucked from wax, and forced herself to speak.

"Jean," she said. "Jean Duprez."

Boyd had already glanced beyond her. She watched him prepare his vague smile for the next person in line and noted that the mention of her full name did not spark his interest. She wasn't sure what she'd expected—a raised eyebrow, a look askance, mock horror, a wink—something, she supposed, that would indicate Claudia had spoken to him about her, but he gave her hand a pallid squeeze and she moved on.

Bland, bland. How could her cousin have married him? Well, it had been years since they'd spent time together; perhaps Claudia was vastly different from the fierce girl she remembered. Her heel caught and she glanced down at the gray cobbles, the rivers of crimson rose petals running between them. Children had been placed across from the bride and groom in a shaft of sunlight, throwing the petals at all the well-wishers; a few blew around her ankles and one clung to her calf.

Someone was standing beside her, waiting for her to go on. A man, she noticed, tall and dark-haired; he seemed to be staring.

The church bells were still ringing, passersby in cars were waving and calling out their congratulations; a flock of pigeons flew low overhead, cooing, their wings beating with a sound like fluttering fabric, and Jean watched them, the way their iridescent necks shone in the sun, until she lost them as they arced around the steeple.

Ahead was the minister, tomato-faced and smiling, and beyond him Sally, Claudia's mother—Jean's aunt. Happiness had the odd effect of making her ugly, it seemed; her face was tear-stained and swollen. She busied herself with a bow at the side of her fussy dress as Jean approached, and Jean thought Sally planned to snub her, but at the last moment Sally turned and gave her a quick, false smile.

"Jean," she said. "So Claudia did invite you." Her voice was full of the old Gallic chilliness, but even aimed at her, Jean found its familiarity oddly reassuring.

"Yes. So nice of her to remember, wasn't it?"

"What beautiful shoes," Sally said, looking down.

"Thank you." Jean lifted one foot and tilted the shoe into sunlight. "Unusual, don't you think? And amazingly comfortable."

"And so last year," Sally said. "I can tell by the straps."

Jean swiftly reached the end of the line.

.   .   .

The reception was at Sally's lake house, with its broad, slop-
ing lawn, where the lush grass was as soft as powder beneath
Jean's shoes, and teal green in the canted afternoon sunlight. A
waiter crossed the grass in front of her, holding aloft a silver tray
of champagne flutes, the glasses flashing in the sun, and Jean
plucked two as he passed; cornered by someone irritatingly per-
sistent, she could wave the extra and claim she had to be off. She
drank half of one, then slipped through the shrubbery to the
shore, thinking that to Claudia, at least, the wedding must have
seemed a grand success. It was warm and sunny, people were
dancing and laughing, and all along the water a sinuous band of
fruit trees were in bloom—crabapple or cherry, Jean thought—
their pink blossoms pale against the black bark of the trunks.
Very late this year; it had been a cold spring.

By the shore stood two men, a boy of about eighteen wearing
a rolled blue bandanna as a headband and an expensive but
stained suit, and beside him, on a rock, a middle-aged man in
bare feet and khaki shorts, wearing a mocha-colored velvet
tuxedo jacket. Both were smoking cigars. She thought they
looked foolish, trying too hard to be hip, and it amused her to
watch and judge, since she knew almost no one at the wedding,

and those she did, she remembered only distantly, from the seemingly endless hours she'd spent along this very shore as a child.

She and Claudia had played daily when they were younger, until they were twelve; their names for each other had been She and Me. Then their parents stopped seeing one another, some argument she barely remembered concerning the two of them, the obsessive nature of their play, their made-up language. It had been an irrevocable break, and now, years later, her cousin had written to her out of the blue and announced she was marrying and wouldn't Jean please come? It would mean so much.

And so here she was. They'd barely had time to say hello, though Jean arrived an hour early for the service, and now the reception was halfway over. Checking her watch, she decided it would be another hour before she could leave gracefully, and when she looked up she glimpsed her aunt's blue dress passing behind the white and coral azaleas, the dress such a beautiful blue, Jean thought, one hardly noticed the gray in Sally's hair against it. She seemed on her way somewhere, as she had all afternoon; the caterers needed checking up on, perhaps. Weddings weren't for the bride and groom, of course, but for their parents, and Sally was ignoring Jean completely and Uncle Teddy was dead, and Boyd's parents seemed merely happy to be there, as if they hadn't quite believed Boyd would pull this off. Boyd. She drank more of the champagne. Even his name sounded foolish.

The cigar smoke from the men beside Jean was heady, too strong, really, but in the warm sunshine she found herself attracted to it and moving closer to its source. Soon her allergies would kick in: her temples would throb, her eyes fill with water, and every breath would become a struggle, but for now the scent was pleasurable. She listened to the buzz of the quiet conversation and wondered briefly if the two men might be her distant relatives, if she'd seen them years ago at family Christmas parties, perhaps made fun of them with Claudia. One year she and Claudia had carved the initials of all their least favorite relatives into her aunt's kitchen wall, a task that had taken half an hour.

Music and echoing laughter reached her from over the water, and she turned to watch the approach of the barge with the bride and groom and many of the guests. They had gone out on it earlier, and now they were dancing to the tunes of a jazz trio, women in pastel dresses floating in the arms of tuxedoed men, their bright, indistinct faces uniformly happy. Jean searched for Claudia and Boyd in the crowd. The barge was right in front of her, at the midpoint of its orbit around the lake, so close she could see the rust-red paint peeling on its hull and hear the quiet chug of its engine below the strains of the music, but even so she couldn't make out the bride and groom. They must have been hidden in the center of the throng, the core of happiness around which the happiness of others gathered, like bees around a honeycomb. Listening to the waltz, an up-tempo number she recalled from dancing lessons long ago, boys' sweaty palms clasping her gloved one, she regretted her decision to stay ashore.

"It wasn't a choice, really," she said, to comfort herself, and when the middle-aged man standing on the rock glanced up and smiled around his cigar, she realized she'd spoken aloud. At work it didn't matter, there they were used to her ways, but among strangers the habit embarrassed her. She felt the rims of her ears redden and finished the first glass of champagne, then turned to face the lake.

She had since childhood harbored a vague foreboding about deep water. It had not kept her from learning to swim, but when she'd been asked earlier to go on the boat it had held her back as surely as a physical restraint, yet she'd made a choice, she knew that. Everything was a choice. Ashore there was champagne, and a long meal of chilled gazpacho and grilled shrimp and smoked salmon, and the buzz of slightly drunken conversation all around her, and she'd chosen safety and satiety over the press of a stranger's hand, urging her to come aboard and dance, though she wouldn't have, younger. She and Claudia had never opted for security as children. They'd squirted trails of lighter fluid on their forearms and lit them; dropped bricks ever nearer to their bare toes from higher and higher, eyes closed, aiming by feel and not by sight; ridden their bicycles down steep, curving hills in utter darkness, their bare, dirty feet propped on the handlebars in order to keep from braking. But all of that seemed long ago.

She worked to dislodge a rock from the shore with the toe of her shoe, continuing at it even after scraping the leather, and toppled it into the water, where the dropped pink blossoms from the fruit trees bobbed in its wake.

Sensing movement nearby, she looked up to see the boy with the headband detach himself from the man, and as he neared, his eyes rose only to her breasts. Her Inappropriate Date Magnet appeared to be on at full force, and she did not bother to stifle her sigh. The magnet had been off, briefly, when she'd been asked to go out on the water, and turning down the stranger's invitation had been foolish. This proved it.

He took the cigar from his mouth, its end sodden and horribly misshapen, as if it was something dredged from the bottom of the lake, and she felt like asking if he knew he wasn't supposed to eat it. When he smiled at her, showing nice teeth, sex was clearly on his mind, but judging by his swagger, it would be of the quick and unmemorable kind.

"Someone as lovely as you shouldn't be lonely," he said, "today of all days."

"I'm not lonely," she said, "just alone. And someone as old as you ought to have a better line."

He blanched, and she realized how she must have sounded, the scolding, dismissive edge to her anger, and she felt a momentary pang of regret, but then she decided she shouldn't care. He'd approached her uninvited, after all, and not the other way around, and the proprietary air he exuded was annoying. Still, it was a wedding, people were in a festive mood. She raised the second champagne flute, still full, by way of explanation. "I'm waiting for someone," she said, hoping to sound diplomatic.

"Obviously not me." His face had lost its color, and his voice was rising to a whine, which irritated her.

"Obviously," she said.

When he turned back, he was so angry that she could almost hear him ticking.

The man relighted the boy's cigar and they leaned together and began to talk. She heard the slight hissing of their words, a snatch of laughter, something guttural like a grunt, and then the man sneered and shook his head. They were discussing her, her skin prickled with the knowledge, and the air in her lungs suddenly thickened, as if she were breathing mud.

She strained to hear the waltz as the barge moved away over the water, but the boy's voice grew louder, almost boasting, and when the man said something to make the boy tilt his head back and laugh and then stared at her over the boy's shaking shoulder, she knew what would happen next; men in pairs were so transparent. She had always hated that, the pack mentality. He slapped the boy's back and came toward her.

It angered her. She hadn't asked for this, why couldn't they let her be? Nonetheless she gave him the full radiance of her smile. She knew it worked; years before, one of her doctors had suggested she smile more. It's free, he said, and inspires people to like you. But I don't want them to like me, she'd replied. I want them to leave me alone.

"I hope my nephew wasn't rude," the man said, holding out a hand. "Austin Harding."

"How do you do." She let him hold her hand longer than required, and when he noticed that, he stepped a foot closer. It did not surprise her that his cologne was *Brut,* or that she could smell it even over the cigar.

"Don't you think it's a perfect evening for a walk?" he said, pointing the cigar at the far end of the lake.

"A walk would be just the thing," she said.

He started along the shore, bare feet padding on the stones, and when she didn't follow he turned back to her and smiled.

"Coming?"

"No. I was hoping you'd just walk away."

Before he could reply, she drained the second glass of champagne and began moving up the lawn, putting a stand of fragrant blooming viburnum between them. In case he followed, thinking of his bare feet, she dropped the flutes in the trampled grass.

A bridesmaid in a lemon-colored dress was talking to an usher, their faces red in the late-afternoon light, and Jean watched them from across the lawn, seated on the grass, the skin across her cheekbones tight from the day's sun, her eyes tired. The woman moved back and forth in front of the usher, talking, animated, and now and again the man nodded or shrugged, but mostly he was impassive, and when he spoke, his responses seemed monosyllabic. After a few minutes the bridesmaid left him, but before going she held up one finger, wagged it, and put her other hand out, urging him to stay. The third time she did it he nodded.

When the bridesmaid returned, holding two white coffee cups on their saucers, the man was gone. She swiveled her head from side to side, then rose up on her toes trying to find him, without luck. Soon she approached another usher in his swallowtail coat and offered the coffee to him.

A man came and stood beside Jean.

"Pitiful, isn't it?" he said.

Jean could not make out his face, as the sun was just above his shoulder, but she gathered he was speaking about the bridesmaid. She wished she hadn't laid her hat beside her on the grass; putting it on now would be too obvious. As it was, she could look no higher than his chest.

"It is rather sad," she said, glancing back across the lawn. The usher held up his hand in refusal of the coffee, and without a word the bridesmaid spun away. A third usher, balding and ponytailed, was making his slow way toward the porch, and the bridesmaid moved to overtake him.

"I suppose if I wore a swallowtail coat, I'd be more popular," the man said to Jean.

"Would you really want to be?"

The man laughed. "No. I think not. That coffee's got to be cold by now, and I can't imagine the conversation is much better. Have you heard her voice?"

Jean said she hadn't.

"She sounds like Gomer Pyle's sister."

Jean shielded her eyes, trying to see his face, and when he shifted, the long straight line of his nose became distinguishable. She had the odd, passing sensation that he enjoyed watching her struggle, which irritated and intrigued her, and she was about to ask him to move when he crouched beside her, steadying himself with one hand on her knee. She still couldn't see his face. When he ducked she'd been left staring into the sun, and now she had to close her eyes and turn away.

"You're Jean, Claudia's cousin." It was not a question. "I'm Steven."

"Steven." On her closed eyelids she saw a single burning sun, yellow against a black background, which after a few seconds bisected into two black balls, the area around them turning orange. She squeezed her eyes to clear her vision.

"Steven Cain."

She opened her eyes and looked at him. The name meant nothing to her, of course, though she didn't let on. He held his hand out, shook hers firmly, then dropped it back on her knee, and she liked that, the ease of his affection. His hand was warm and dry and lighter than she would have guessed, as if it were stuffed with feathers, but his touch felt vital and electric.

"Claudia's told me quite a bit about you. I hope you won't think me too forward. You're the one person I hoped to meet from the entire party."

"How flattering." She meant it, pleased that Claudia had spoken of her, and she became aware of her dress clinging to her chest and thighs in the heat, as if the day had suddenly grown hotter. She breathed deeply to calm herself, taking in the smell of crushed grass and the scent of his cologne, which was unusual, a blend of smells and colors, cinnamon and sienna and burnt amber, she thought, something ancient and earthy and enduring. The exoticism made it attractive. His shoes were tightly woven flats, made of buttery leather.

"Good thing you found me now," she said. "I'm afraid I was getting ready to leave."

"Yes, I thought you might be. I let it go rather too long, didn't I?" He shook his head at his own foolishness. "I knew if I didn't come over now I'd lose my chance."

"You don't seem the shy type."

"Oh." He waved dismissively. "I'm not."

When he lifted his hand from her knee it was as if her skin had been peeled away, she felt suddenly exposed, and she wished he'd put it back.

"To be honest," he said, shifting his weight from one leg to the other, "I was watching you for a while."

"Oh really?" She slid her hands down her calves and grasped her ankles, folding herself in half. Her cheek rested on her knee, where the smooth skin was still warm from his touch.

"To be sure." He nodded, looking out over the lake, the bright plane of copper-colored water. "Claudia said you were unusual, but one never knows."

"You mean, I might have been like that bridesmaid."

"Exactly."

Now it was her turn to laugh. She leaned back on her palms, wondering how long he'd been watching, and what exactly he'd seen. "And I passed?" She worked her fingers into the warm grass until they reached dirt.

"Certainly. I should have trusted Claudia."

From beside him he produced a glass of champagne, strings of thin bubbles rising to its surface.

"I'd offer to get you one," he said.

"But you're afraid I'd leave?"

"No." He sipped the champagne, and she watched his throat move as he swallowed, and then he pressed the glass into the grass near her feet. He seemed to inspect her shoes, the complicated straps enveloping her arches and ankles, the scrape across the right one. "I'm sure you wouldn't. I believe everything Claudia's told me is true. You're an only child, like Claudia, and you two share the same birthday, don't you, like twins?"

Jean nodded.

"So you're not a flirt. She said you wouldn't be. But you will be leaving the party soon, and you don't want to get hurt. You have to drive."

"And you don't?"

"I'm an overnight guest."

"A slumber party. I didn't know. I'd have wangled an invitation."

He pulled back a bit, as if offended, and tensed his jaw, but she wasn't sure what she'd said wrong; beginnings were always so rocky. Of course, she'd found that endings could be even worse: Oliver Brisbane had called her for five or six months after she'd broken up with him, discovering her number each time though she changed it continually and had it unlisted, and always he left the same message, "Brisbane calling. I'll try again." Eventually he'd given up, but by then she'd met Pavel Hammond, whom she thought might be the one, until the night she'd awoken to find him sitting on the floor beside her bed, watching her sleep, the planes of his angular Slavic face distinct, pale wedges in the dark. He'd climbed the fire escape to reach her.

She shivered at the memory, those tiny, dark eyes, then touched Steven's arm. "You must live a long way off."

He drank the rest of his champagne, observing her hand on his arm, and put the glass down beside her calf. She realized she'd been watching him closely, studying him, really, because she sensed that she could not afford to make a mistake this time. At last he stood, and from his face he seemed to have reached a decision.

She shielded her eyes again, looking up at him, her pulse throbbing at her temples and throat. His hair was short and very black, but she couldn't see his eyes, and she still didn't have a good mental picture of his face. She did not want him to leave.

"I live nearer the city." He produced a small pair of nickel-plated binoculars from a jacket pocket, turned them over in his hands, and pocketed them again. "I have a boat."

She looked toward the docks, the swaying, forested masts, where halyards were clanking against the aluminum and a few gulls sat perched high up among the flapping pennants and flags.

"Not here. On the ocean, just north of Boston. I'd like you to come out on it with me. Do you sail? That's the one thing Claudia didn't tell me."

Her stomach hollowed at the thought, just a few boards between her and all that water, but she did not allow herself to contemplate it, or why her desire for his presence reminded her—vaguely, but insistently—of other desires she could not at the moment name.

"I haven't sailed," she said. The briefest of pauses, she barely knew him, yet Claudia had spoken to him about her, and he had sought her out. "But I'd love to."

"Good. You'll hear from me next week, then. I look forward to it."

"As do I."

He bent over her. Perhaps he would touch her shoulder; her skin tingled in anticipation, and she believed she could distinguish each freckle and pore, and that, after, she'd be able to recall the exact spot on which his fingers had rested.

But he straightened. "You'll be a natural on the water." With his shoe he tapped the glass he'd left behind, making it ring. "You might take that, in case anyone else bothers you."

That he'd been watching her so long surprised her. She'd been about to give him her phone number, which was unlisted again, but by the time she recovered he'd turned and walked away. She started to reach out after him, stifled the gesture, took up her hat, stood, and smoothed her dress while she watched him go.

The wedding photographer had come upon them and snapped a few shots. He caught the motion of her reaching hand, and though Jean never saw the picture, Claudia did, yet it was the one he'd taken earlier, just before Steven stepped away, that Claudia would always remember. It showed the two of them in profile, Jean seated on the grass and Steven looming above her, the long swell of the lake rising between them, their faces blotted out by the sun. The barge with the dancers had just floated into the top of the frame, black because it was backlit, and it seemed to be a mistake in the photograph or a flaw in the negative, a dead spot. This was the one picture from her own wedding that Claudia never forgot.

She threw out the print early on, even before her divorce, but its image appeared to her quite often, especially during the warm days of late spring when the spicy vanilla scent of viburnum drifted into her open bedroom window and the afternoon sunlight slanted across the maple floorboards, turning them a butterscotch orange. At night, dreaming, she saw herself taking the picture, though of course that was impossible. When it had been snapped, she'd been far out on the lake, dancing over the placid water.

HE DID NOT PHONE ON MONDAY OR TUESDAY. WEDNESDAY, determined not to think about him, Jean left her office at lunch for a new Thai restaurant across town, then hurried back without eating—despising herself for doing so—convinced she'd miss his call; Claudia must have told him where she worked. Thursday she decided that the champagne had given him false courage and that he'd come to regret his boldness, and by Friday she was certain that his change of heart no longer bothered her. In celebration, she wore a new perfume to work, *Savoir,* which to her seemed both subtle and distinctive—one noticed it only if one stood close to her, but then its crisp citrus scent was unmistakable. She found herself sniffing the insides of her wrists to take it in.

In the early afternoon, a slack time, she doodled over the cover of a folder on her desk, and, studying the markings, saw that she'd written Steven's name dozens of times, the initial double loops of the *S,* the jagged *t,* the near circles of the vowels. She called the receptionist to ask if anyone had left her a message, and after being told for the second time that no one had, she began to hate her office.

It was spare and elegant, nearly bare of decoration, and she'd fought to keep it that way, throwing out the occasional plant or poster coworkers gave her around holidays, and refusing her boss's standing offer to replace the simple wooden and metal trestle table she worked on with something "more refined." From Bonnie, she knew, that would mean a desk both massive and ornate. But now the room's cell-like qualities oppressed her: it was small, it smelled of chemicals, and it had no window, nothing to catch her eye and distract her restless mind from turning in on itself. Some of her old work hung on the walls—her first successful ads, framed in unfinished wood—and she understood now that all of it was stupid, obvious and shallow and dull, a poor imitation of work others had done earlier and better. What was there in it that distinguished it, that distinguished her? Nothing. That she'd thought it fit to mount galled her, she could imagine it being laughed at.

She tried to recall the scent of crushed grass, the feel of champagne bubbles bursting against the roof of her mouth, the color of Steven's eyes, but all of the sensations were faded and indistinct, like images in sun-bleached pictures. Rubbing the spot on her knee where he had touched her, she smudged her blouse with a drafting pencil, and when she flicked at the leaden smear to clean it, managed only to work it deeper into the fabric. Cursing, she turned back to her desk, where the comps for the Pettigrew account—due on Monday and almost finished—were stacked in leaning piles. They depressed her. Fat, clumsy bodies, a nearly invisible product logo, sloppily done letters; she was meant to create the ads, not execute them, and here was the all-too-obvious proof.

She folded one of the drawings in half, in quarters, in eighths, and she was tearing it neatly along the folds when she smelled patchouli and looked up to find Bonnie standing in the doorway, holding a stack of files. Patchouli had a dusty, androgynous smell that Jean hated; it reminded her of the attics she'd played in as a child, and of her Aunt Sally.

"Plans this weekend, Jean?" Bonnie said, miming a knock and entering.

Jean had disliked Bonnie upon first meeting her, a feeling whose origins she traced to the scent and whose strength had never abated, and now she watched Bonnie stop in front of the desk and put on a smile. Being pleasant was something Bonnie was working at, remembering to ask after her coworkers' lives before launching into whatever it was she really wanted. Jean had seen the tattered management book stuffed into Bonnie's purse: *Connections to Success, The Human Verbal Touch Is Business Magic.*

"Yes. I'm afraid so," Jean said. "I do have plans."

"Oh really?" Bonnie lowered the files to her side and fiddled with her necklace, a gaudy silver thing whose pendants rattled at her touch. Jean guessed from the awkward pause it was not the answer Bonnie had expected. "What might those be?"

Haven't got to the "Workers Who Give Surprising Answers" chapter yet, have we? Jean thought. She swiveled in her chair.

"Sailing." She'd been preparing to let people know all week, and it pleased her to hear the word come out sounding so smoothly indifferent.

"Sailing?"

"Yes."

"Down to the river? At the place with lessons?" Bonnie sat, face brightening, and Jean remembered that Bonnie had given her a flyer the year before from an outfit along the esplanade that offered lessons. "RANK (BUT NOT RANK!) BEGINNERS TO ABLE-BODIED SEA PEOPLE!" *Who wrote these things?* she wondered. Bonnie had wanted the whole office to go, as a way to bond with her, the new boss; Jean alone had demurred.

"God no," Jean said. She wanted to look out a window, but

she stared instead at the blank wall opposite her open door and picked out strands of color glinting in the textured paper that covered it. Forest green, sky blue, perhaps a bit of indigo. "Nothing like that. On a friend's boat."

Bonnie leaned toward Jean's desk, smiling, red lipstick slanting across one canine. The files were in her lap now, forgotten. "An old friend?" Her voice was lowered, her head cocked, as if Jean might whisper her response.

"New."

Bonnie raised her eyebrows, expectant, but Jean smiled back resolutely, unwilling to say more. A phone began to ring in one of the outer offices, four rings, five rings, six, and after it stopped Bonnie sat back and tapped the files on her thighs with the fingernails of both hands. "Well," she said. "Sounds exciting. I won't weigh you down with these." She winked and gathered up the files and stood. "You'll have plenty to do, I guess."

"Thank you," Jean said. "And if you don't mind, I'd like to leave a little early today."

Bonnie paused before answering, and Jean leaned forward and whispered, "Supplies."

Bonnie's face flushed, probably with pleasure, all the way up to the fine lines around her eyes, the added color causing her foundation makeup to look caked.

"Fine, Jean, go right ahead. I've often said you should make more time for yourself. Take the whole afternoon if you need it."

At the door she turned, and Jean's stomach sank. She knew what was coming next: Bonnie would wish her luck, or giggle conspiratorially, or ask her to provide her with all the juicy details on Monday—something unsophisticated and girlish.

"You'll have time to polish up the Pettigrew drawings?" she said.

Surprised, Jean could only nod.

"Monday's meeting is at one," Bonnie said. "But don't you worry too much about it. I can see from your desk you've made a good start on them."

Jean understood: Bonnie meant to remind her that her visit had been supervisory, not social; she'd been foolish to think otherwise.

"And besides," Bonnie said, "other things sometimes come first, in time if not in importance. Enjoy being with Steven." She rapped on the door frame and left.

Jean covered up Steven's name to keep others from noticing it, and listened to Bonnie's footsteps grow fainter as she moved down the carpeted hall. They stopped shortly, and then Jean heard Bonnie whispering to one of the other art directors. About her, no doubt. She leaned forward and turned her ear to listen, but it was no use: she couldn't distinguish Bonnie's words, only the sound of her voice, rustling like a squirrel in leaves as she spoke.

Saturday, Jean went into the office and devoted herself to the Pettigrew drawings. They were not perfect when she was done, which annoyed her, but she had nearly succeeded in stripping the lettering to something elemental—the suggestion of letters rather than the letters themselves—which would be enough for Bonnie to play up and make a selling point. A hint, nothing obvious, that was Pettigrew's signature look; Jean knew because she had created it.

Home, she cooked herself dinner, cleaned the apartment, and leafed through her copy of *Plummerman's Collecting Guide,* and then at midnight called Claudia, but the phone rang unanswered for a full three minutes and after that she gave up and unplugged it. She slept with her windows open, as she always had, though she knew Mrs. Olsen, her elderly neighbor, disapproved. Two or three times a month she slipped notes and news clippings into Jean's mailbox, the folded notes illegible and the news clippings detailing burglaries and robberies in the area—once a murder— and across the accompanying photographs she had crayoned COULD BE YOU! in big green block letters. But no one was going to climb five stories to get Jean; they'd have to go up the brick, since the apartment, alone of the ones in the building, didn't have a fire escape.

An oversight, the landlord had told Jean when she first looked at the place, mistaking her surprise for fear. He had knocked his cigarette ash into his cupped palm as they walked from room to room and assured her that it would soon be fixed, but the code violation didn't scare Jean, it was the reason she chose the apartment. She was not afraid of fire, and as the main entrance to the building was off an alley, not the street, she believed that here, at least, her privacy would be guaranteed. She would not awake to find that Pavel Hammond had climbed all that way to watch her sleep.

Sunday, Jean awoke in the dark to humid air and clinging sheets. She kicked them off and lay sweating on the bed, staring at the plaster ceiling until its cracks became visible and a Creamsicle orange rim of dawn began to show in the eastern sky. The phone was beside her and she was glad she'd unplugged it; if Steven hadn't called by now, he wasn't going to. A shower, some coffee and a roll, and then she was off, to Marblehead, her usual Sunday-morning routine.

In Marblehead, the air was salty, the wind onshore, and she slipped her sweater on, surprised by the chill. The water was different, she reminded herself, it changed things; that was a lesson she had to learn again and again. She had a few hundred dollars cash, her wallet, a checkbook in case anything at the flea market caught her fancy; she never lost hope that it might.

The steep harborside streets were still blue with morning shade, and as she traversed them she surveyed the flea market, its tables of junk and treasure, its vendors, its crowd. She'd arrived early, but others had come even earlier, and many were already leaving, some holding pictureless frames and others looking like refugees from a waterfront disaster as they passed her, clutching chairs or lamps or carrying the drawers from desks and bureaus under their arms or across their shoulders, and she had to reassure herself that she'd missed nothing. They were decorators, mostly, with their measuring tapes and their bottled water, and big items always went quickly, she knew; getting there after they'd gone made her task easier—less jostling, fewer fights over who saw something first. She was interested chiefly in pens.

Her first time through was just an inspection, as it was best not to show even a flicker of attraction. She was young or at least youngish, her hair was thick and glossy, she was nearly six feet tall, and she knew most of the vendors would remember her having passed—especially this early, when the crowds had not yet arrived. She noted a stall displaying some kind of handmade dogs and marked its location and half an hour later, walking uphill this time, came back. It was a little warmer; she could feel herself beginning to sweat, the sun was on her neck. A flowering crab in a corner yard had spread its bloom, the white blossoms giving off an overripe scent and scattering across the lawn like snow in a sudden breeze.

The dogs had been made from partially melted sugar cubes, awkwardly glued together and painted in fluorescent colors—green, yellow, orange—and, jumbled about, they resembled piles of gravel lining the bottom of fish tanks. Only a few dogs were able to stand, the rest lay on their sides, their misshapen feet misserving them, and she picked one up, blue and longish, with a black Magic Marker tip for a nose and long, hanging ears. The tail had a small Styrofoam ball stuck on its end; its stomach crumbled in her palm.

"That is a poodle," the vendor said, enunciating each word. She was a middle-aged woman with dyed blond hair and an enormous, swollen-looking chest. Her blouse was too tight, pinching the skin on her arms, and for some reason she was holding a hammer.

"Standard poodle," she said. "Built exactly to scale."

"It's unusual," Jean said.

"Yes it is. It certainly is that." The woman's voice crackled as she spoke, as if she was breathing through cellophane. "I had to make it a she-dog. Trying to melt little wiener shapes is too hard."

Putting it down, Jean was careful not to let it touch the others, afraid one of its legs might scrape off. "Did you make it?"

"Took three days. That smile is the real thing. You find yourself a standard poodle and tell me it isn't. They're smart dogs. On all the tests, they're number two."

At the next table, another vendor had placed an old cigar box; it was lying open, filled with pens. She had been right, then. Cloisonné, crystal, a few silver, and one gold, which gleamed beneath the others; she was mindful not to look. That was the cardinal rule of the market, not to display your interest, otherwise you spooked your prey—prices doubled or tripled, sometimes items suddenly weren't for sale, artificial scarcities were created and bidding could start; she would not allow herself to be the one to set it off.

"They certainly are stunning," she said of the dogs. "But I'm afraid I have nowhere to display them in my apartment."

The woman's face changed, as if Jean had insulted her, and she reached over the table with the hammer and pulled the poodle back toward the others with the claw.

"You shouldn't handle them, then. I wouldn't have let you if I'd known that was all you were about."

She crossed her arms below her chest, as if to give her breasts something to rest on, and turned away. The vendor next to her, leaning against the tailgate of his truck, tall, wearing blue jeans and a blue-and-white striped shirt, was smiling. Jean saw his straight, even teeth from the corner of her eye and realized that touching the dog had been a miscalculation; now she would have to wait until after lunch to look at his pens.

The café had a few tables with umbrellas outside on a cobbled stretch of sidewalk bordered by a white picket fence, but Jean was the only one brave enough to sit out in the wind. She cupped her cold fingers around her mug of hot chocolate, and when they warmed enough for her to feel them, she reached into her purse for her cheese sandwich. She ate quickly, worried that someone from the office might see her, though she'd rehearsed her story in case it should be Bonnie. She'd mixed up her weekends, that was all—it was during the one to come that she was supposed to sail.

Far out in the harbor, sailboats were passing beyond the breakwater. They looked insubstantial, pieces of Styrofoam flung on the surface of a lake. She picked one boat to follow and watched it glide out to sea until it dropped below the horizon, and just as it disappeared a fat white cloud drifted in front of the sun and the light changed, the green water turned black, and the smell of the sea grew suddenly stronger. She was glad Steven hadn't called. What on earth had made her think she'd like to go out on the water? Above her, the loose fabric of the umbrella snapped in the rising wind.

The sun came out again and she checked her watch—it was nearly noon and shadows were disappearing. Houses had west windows open, the fair should have been filling up, but the crowd was actually thinning. A desultory pace lent the day the feel of a holiday weekend in the city, when the only people left in the emptied streets reminded her of the old pieces of furniture abandoned by people when they move. Jean, wondering if perhaps the east wind had driven everyone inland, was glad not to have to fight crowds, but the lack of people also presented a danger: she would not be able to wait as long as she wanted since the vendors might close up early. She returned to the stall that displayed the pens.

Lifting things, she said, "How much is this? And this? And this?" but did not listen to the vendor's replies. Canary-yellow Fiesta ware, a German beer stein, a glass cutter that felt heavy and surprisingly imbalanced in her palm. The pens were the fourth thing she handled. Some days she made the item she wanted the third thing, some days the fifth, and some days she wouldn't even ask, leaving whatever she wanted for another trip. On those occasions, when she returned, she'd offer half the asking price. As she spoke, the woman with the melted-sugar dogs glared at her.

"And this pen?" She held up a cloisonné pen, a good one, even the pocket clip had been enameled. It was smooth and clean-lined, balanced and thin and well made, and it had a *G* stamped on the flat end of the cap.

"Ten dollar," he said. His English was not very strong, Italian, she guessed. His skin was tanned, lined, his fingers were broad and stained, the thick nails opaque. He might have been a farmer.

She put the pen back and held up an inferior one, a Parker, some of the cloisonné was missing, and raised her eyebrows.

"Fifteen."

"Why the difference?"

"Works," he said. Taking the pen from her, he uncapped it, then spit in his palm and dragged the nib through the spittle to show her. A spidery trail of blue ink began to cross his callused skin.

So he did not know the relative value of his pens, a good thing.

He wiped his palm and the nib on his jeans and held out both ends of the pen to her. "You want? You try?"

She shook her head and fingered through the other pens, then picked up the stein again and read the name stamped on the bottom: Schnitzengruber. "Where's this from?"

He shrugged. "Wife's. We no use." He put the pen back and flipped the box lid closed, which meant he was smarter than she'd allowed for; she would have to declare her interest now by re-opening it. She thought of simply walking away, but the pens appeared in her mind's eye, the gold Cross, the black enamel Mont Blanc, the two sapphire Watermans. Most of the others were worthless, cheaper Kronos or Parkers, which had never worked well when they'd been new and which now would bleed and gum. The first cloisonné she'd held was probably a Grieshaber. Though she'd read about them she'd never seen one, and she'd reached for it instinctively, which she thought might work in her favor—one never touched first what one really desired, so her undisciplined impulsiveness might serve to mislead him.

Her sense that here at last was that rare something worthy of her interest, which therefore she had to have, was, she realized, what she'd been feeling about Steven at her cousin's wedding, the feeling she'd been unable to recall. But he hadn't felt the same way, obviously; he hadn't phoned, he hadn't written, he hadn't appeared magically on her doorstep.

She forced herself to put him from her mind and reopened the box and picked up the gold Cross. Its nib was wide, a full stub, and she'd have to replace it if she was going to use the pen; she tended to make her letters sharper than that nib would allow. For a matching gold nib, that meant another seventy-five dollars at the start.

"And this?"

He waited for her to look up and she was sure she knew why. Years before, she'd read that Arab traders, bargaining, watched your eyes, and once your pupils narrowed they were certain you had reached the price you were willing to pay and they would refuse to go any lower. Vendors throughout the various fairs seemed aware of that folklore; they were always watching her eyes.

"One hundred dollar," he said.

She didn't blink. "That's absurd."

She tried the two Watermans without listening to his prices.

He picked up the Cross again.

"Real gold. Is worth monies."

"Fifty," she said, letting him see her eyes. It was probably one of the 1920s series, with a vacuum filling system and twin ink reservoirs, for which she'd been prepared to go up to two hundred dollars, but he wouldn't be able to detect that. For a few days after she'd heard about the Arabs' methods, every time she passed a mirror she had stopped to stare at her reflection and begun to lie, telling a whole string of them, rapidly. *I like my job, Winter is my favorite season, I want to die old and decrepit.* Then she would slip in one statement that was true—*My aunt's house burned down*, or, *Red is a color*, or, *My uncle was badly burned*—and then she would lie again, as many lies as she could think of, quickly, and it was true: the truth narrowed her eyes. With practice, however, over many months, she found that she could hide the truth, give nothing away. The trick was a second voice in her head, midway in register between her own voice and Claudia's, background to her other thoughts, repeating the same three words, over and over. *It's a lie, it's a lie, it's a lie.* The chant soothed her, put her in a kind of trance, and she heard it now running in the back of her mind.

At sixty dollars his eyes narrowed and he crossed his arms.

"Throw in this one," she said, holding up the Grieshaber, "and you have a deal."

He stuck at sixty-five. For another ten she bought a Waterman, and for twenty more she got the Mont Blanc.

After she paid, he swept his cupped hand over the entire display, palm up.

"Other than pen, five dollar for anything on table."

He wanted to make it an even hundred, but she would not oblige him. "No. Just the pens today. And I've already bought too much." She held up the pens as proof before tucking them into her bag. It would be months before she could check his stock again, which she felt sure he would replenish; if she bought even one more now, he'd probably do some research and never again get taken.

She snapped her purse shut and turned away, and heard the lady with the sugar dogs muttering, "What, you can display pens but not my dogs?"

Jean ignored her. Did the woman not know that this was how the market worked? Every vendor had a perfect buyer, someone out there waiting to find her. Today had been someone else's day. Her day would come, someone would seek her out and surprise her with the strength of his interest, but if she did not wait for it, she would not do well.

When she got home there was a single message on her answering machine, a woman's voice, older and halting.

"This is Celia Barnes," she said. "I was at Miss May's funeral today."

Then came a long pause and Jean reached to erase it, but just before she pressed the button the woman's voice returned.

"That was the prettiest casket I have ever seen, and I was interested in finding out how I might get one for myself. Could you call me at home?" After giving her number, she hung up.

Jean played it back once, pretending the cryptic message was for her, though she knew it wasn't. Her number was one digit off from that of a nearby funeral parlor, and every couple of weeks she got calls meant for it, usually a family member elected or left to handle funeral arrangements, thinking that he or she had reached the home. Sometimes in the background, during the pauses, would come the incoherent echoes of other conversations, warped and mysterious and strangely troubling. They attracted Jean. After listening to dozens of them, she had decided they sounded like the querulous voices of the dead, anxious to communicate preferences about their own funerals, angered by their inability to do so. Today there weren't any echoes.

She cleaned the pens with ammonia and silver nitrate, and then filled their bladders with black ink. She'd been right about the Cross, its unwieldy nib. The Grieshaber worked on the third try. She wrote her name out with each, first with her right hand, then with her left, though it was difficult to tell which was which because in all of them her script was hardly legible; she'd always hated her hand. When she was done she made places for the pens in the silver chest she'd bought for just that purpose, sliding them smoothly into their new velvet homes.

Monday was gray and cold. Clouds hung low and ragged just above the flat rooftops, and then a fog rolled in, smelling of the sea, and the bricks outside her windows seemed to sweat in the opaque mist. Conversations on the street reached Jean with odd distortions, their volume swelling as people moved away, shrinking as they came closer, and she heard someone talking about the daily number. 5511, she repeated, 5511. Jean called in sick, not up to work, to having to bubble about her weekend. Yes, the Pettigrew drawings were done, they were in a file on her desk. No, she didn't think she needed to be at the meeting. She turned off the phone and went back to bed.

On her sheet was a nickel-sized spot of blood. She had started. That she hadn't put in a tampon she took as a sign of depression, as she was more regular than the moon, twenty-eight days and the floodgates opened, five days more and they closed. She tended to feel the onset in her ankles and knees, but the night before she'd attributed her soreness to extra walking at the fair.

She changed the sheets and showered and dressed in sweats, but found herself chilled the entire day, even with the heat up and two pairs of warm woolen socks and extra blankets on the bed; during most of it she slept.

In the afternoon, she opened her eyes at the sound of the mailman's booted steps in the alley. The light was still gray, her mouth tasted like tin, the skin under her eyes felt pouchy, and though her cramps had dulled they had not disappeared. She listened to the familiar rhythm of mail delivery, the heavy outside door squeaking open, the mailman's trudging steps on the stairs, the mailboxes clanging open, the mail thunking as it dropped in, and then the same sounds in reverse order: the closing boxes, his tread on the stairs, the swinging door on its rusty hinge, and his steps again, fading down the alley. He said hello to someone and they became involved in a low, murmuring conversation; their voices were hypnotic. She listened to them, running her tongue over her teeth, and drifted again into sleep.

Later, she awoke as if to the same set of occurrences, steps in the alley, the door swinging open, muffled footsteps on the carpeted stairs, and something dropping into a mailbox. She sat up and listened. The steps came again, the door hinge creaked, the steps moved away, but they didn't sound booted, and soon they disappeared. She realized she was awake and didn't think she'd been dreaming: she could smell bacon. She wrapped a robe around herself and went downstairs.

Mrs. Olsen shuffled to her door as Jean passed, slippers whispering over the worn linoleum floor, and Jean could feel her presence through the door's thin wood. By the mailboxes, the smell of salt air was pungent—the walls seemed soaked in it—and the wooden handrail was gummy to the touch. A letter had come for Jean, mixed in with the bills, her name done in block printing on an unstamped envelope, which she was sure was from Steven. And it was.

The three-page, handwritten letter contained meticulous directions for reaching his boat. *Turn right out of your alley onto Newberry Street and then left on Clarendon Street,* it began, and ended with an invitation in the form of a declarative fragment: *Sailing, Sunday, 5/5, noon.* Underneath were a few personalized lines. He apologized for the delay, something had come up, he promised she would enjoy it. The third time she read the letter she realized with a jolt of approval that he'd used a fountain pen to write it, and that he had a beautiful hand.

There was no number to call; he expected her to go. Holding the envelope to her nose, she found no trace of his cologne. She showered again, and dressed, and poured herself a scotch for company and then began to cook, sautéing white onions for a sauce, leaving the letter lying open on the table, the paper so white it seemed to glow. She thought it sweet that he'd taken such care with the directions, measuring the distance to each turn, detailing landmarks on the way to her destination, which, as it turned out, was The Anchorage, a yacht club in Marblehead. It was similar to, though not the same as, the route she'd taken to Marblehead the day before, so she knew much of it by heart. Over the rest of it, he'd been so precise, it would almost be like going home.

JEAN MET HIM AT THE DOCK WITH A BASKET. CHILLED CAR-
rot and ginger soup, curried chicken with currants and apricot
jam, marinated artichokes, two bottles of Alsatian wine. She'd
also packed cheeses, Stilton and St. André, some champagne
grapes and nectarines, and a strawberry-rhubarb crisp; the bread
was the city's best. She'd splurged on new sunglasses, taking two
hours to choose them, and her hair was tied in a Hermès scarf,
but Steven stood at the end of the boat—stern, it's called, she reminded herself, not wanting to sound ignorant—and didn't invite her aboard.

"How were my directions?" He hadn't shaved and seemed
surprised to see her; his hair was uncombed, his eyes reddened
with sleep, and he was standing with the white insides of his
pants pockets turned out, looking as though he'd been person-
ally ransacked.

"Perfect." And they had been, down to the particular number
of steps his boat lay beyond the clam shack, the turn at the nar-

row turquoise-colored house, the three large potholes she needed to look out for on a curving stretch of Route 1. Driving, she'd seen the name *Jean* spray-painted on a bridge stanchion, green against the orange rusting metal, and though the paint was faded, she'd taken it as an auspicious sign.

"Good." He put both hands to his back and stretched and made a noise in his throat. "I thought you'd be a little later."

The invitation had said noon and coming early had been a mistake, she saw that now, it displayed a certain eagerness. She checked her watch and shrugged; it was a quarter to. "I didn't want to hold you up. I imagine you like to sail on time."

"Yes, that's true." He smiled at her, bobbing up and down with the swell, and the effect was to make him look younger than she'd remembered, a boy bouncing with nerves. How old was he, anyway? She knew nothing about him.

"You know me well. Punctuality is important."

Still, he made no move to welcome her, and she was beginning to think she'd been foolish to spend a half hour standing before her open closet, wondering what to wear, considering that his clothes were so rumpled and ill-fitting they looked borrowed or found.

"Listen," he said. "Do you mind waiting just a minute?" He

gestured at his face and clothes. "I want to clean up, and the boat's not quite ready."

She held the basket out, let it drop back against her thighs. What other options did she have? "Go right ahead."

She waited on the dock. The light was blinding, even with her sunglasses, but at first it was pleasant watching people ready other boats to sail. Engines started and reversed, footsteps rattled the dock's weathered boards, the smells of oil and seaweed and salt air drifted around her. Some of the slips were already empty, and eventually she turned her attention to the harbor, to the wakes of departing boats splitting apart like fish being filleted, to the floating, undulating circular rainbows of spilled fuel, and to the water rising and falling and rising again against the green-scummed pilings of the dock.

An elderly woman dressed in a saffron-yellow pantsuit passed by, limping on her right leg toward the office, her skin lined like a walnut. More lines appeared as she flashed Jean a brief smile. The day grew warmer, the basket too heavy, and Jean let it rest by her feet and looked at Steven's boat, whose name was *Nellie B* and whose hull was painted a glossy marine blue to the waterline, a color she approved of, though it was too dazzling to look at for long. The hull squeaked as it rubbed against the bumpers—bald tires nailed to the dock—and now and again the boat rocked furiously, as if Steven was belowdecks, running back and forth and slamming into the sides.

Ten minutes later, the woman with the walnut face came back, her right leg swinging out in a semicircle as she walked, as if her hip was hinged rather than jointed, and this time she raised her eyebrows at Jean, who shrugged, then pretended to be interested in another boat's rigging. She listened to the woman's awkward footsteps fade down the planking, wondering if perhaps it was inappropriate to stand so long in front of someone's boat; she did not know the proper body language for the docks. But when the woman began openly watching her, hands fisted on her hips, Jean took out Steven's letter and began to reread his directions, which had been scrupulously correct.

Six left turns, fourteen right ones, twenty-six-and-a-half miles altogether, and looking at them now, she realized that after the three streets from her own neighborhood, not one of the streets was named; everything was described in terms of mileage and landmarks.

2.2 miles farther on, you'll see an abandoned center-fireplace colonial on your left, a billboard in front an-

4 9

*nouncing a new development. Two stories, red with black
shutters. Turn right down the road just past it. Go through
three stoplights. The next intersection is busy: a Hess station on the north-east corner, six gas bays, a YMCA (its
sign missing the C) on the southwest, another left here.
Exactly one mile later are three brick warehouses in a row,
the first two empty, all on your left. The third has a white
sign with black lettering, Peterboro Metal Works. On a
windy day you might miss it. The sign is made of ¼″ ply-
wood and lifts parallel to the ground in a stiff breeze. Wait
for the wind to die down if you don't see it.
A sharp right just after it, and get up some speed. With
a stick shift, the short hill at the top could make you stall.*

How had he known she drove a stick? Her Saab did have a
tendency to stall at lights, especially on hills, but it was a courtesy, really, that note about shifting, he probably had these directions handy for anyone who drove up from the city; she'd
been foolish to think that in writing them he'd troubled himself
with her. She refolded the directions and pocketed them, angry
at herself for having misread him.

The woman in the saffron-colored suit was gone, and so was
her boat—the *Lucky Lady*; it was time for Jean to leave, too. She

was feeling progressively more foolish, as if she'd awoken from a daze and found herself a supplicant at some strange altar, involved in rituals she did not understand. No, that was wrong, she thought—she had chosen to be here, but she had not chosen to be abandoned. He would figure out what had happened when he discovered she was gone. She wondered: should she leave the basket, or simply dump its contents on the dock?

She bent to pick it up and a door slid closed on the boat, followed by the click of a latch and three quick footsteps, and when she stood he was smiling above her, hair combed, face shaven, eyes clear and wide open, his clothes looking freshly pressed.

"Sorry I'm a little slow."

"A little?" She straightened her shoulders. "I wouldn't like to see a lot." She was aware that her voice sounded shrill.

He laughed, showing his bright teeth. "I suppose time seems slower when you're waiting. I probably would have left, myself, but I'm glad you didn't."

He held his hand out to help her aboard. "I apologize. Sincerely. And I won't give you cause to be angry again. At least not today."

She felt disarmed, which rankled her, since she couldn't very well comment on his rudeness now without sounding petulant, and yet he was the one who should be uncomfortable, not she. His skin was red, as if he'd scrubbed it roughly, and he rose a foot higher as a swell rocked the boat, then dropped back closer to her level, his arm still extended.

She shifted the basket from hand to hand, letting him wait long enough to notice, then passed it over, took his hand, and climbed aboard. His cologne was noticeably strong and seemed already familiar. He tucked the basket into a locker, steered her around a bound sail to the stern, and pressed a button to start the engine.

"Ready to go?"

She nodded, determined to put her anger behind her.

He held out an orange life jacket. "Would you like one?"

She shook her head, and though by his face she knew she'd made the right decision, when he stowed the life jacket beside her, she memorized its location.

For a few minutes he was too busy to speak, untying lines, pushing off from the dock, steering past the crowded jetty, which was long and made of stone and curved like a scythe. A group of fishermen waved, mostly children, one blond boy skipping a flat stone across their bow, and occasionally Steven gripped her upper arms and repositioned her when he needed to get by, his touch neither flirtatious nor cold. He was simply indifferent to her presence—she might have been a mannequin in his way— and she sat, finally, to give him room, but misjudged the rising seat, which struck her hard enough to bruise.

As they passed the breakwater, he noted the time on a chart. Soon the swells picked up, the hull bounced over waves, and now and then a fine spray sprinkled her skin. The bouncing did not bother her stomach, though she gripped a cushion tight enough to pull the fabric, and she made herself rest her hands on her lap, telling herself to trust in the strength of boards. Gulls followed, circling, screeching, but turned back when it became apparent they would not be fed.

She let herself be lulled by the rhythm of the boat moving over the water and watched the gulls shrink into small black specks in the sky and then vanish, the land sink into the horizon. She could almost taste the salt air. It coated her skin and made her hair feel thick and tangled, and she decided that she had been right to come along.

He looked ahead, as if aiming the bow at some invisible land-mark on the surface of the water, and she tried unsuccessfully to see what he might be using. Why steer toward one swell and not another? She turned back. His shirt was rippling in the wind, and something about his profile, the straight forehead and close-hauled, jibing, but they were all exotic and meant nothing to her. After a while, seeing that she wasn't listening, he stopped.

"I'm sorry," he said, color appearing on both cheeks. "I'm boring you."

"Don't be. It's really quite interesting." His embarrassment pleased her, since it meant he liked her, and she hadn't been bored; she'd been listening to the tone of his voice rather than to his words, letting its sound wash over her, the loving obsessive lilt given to names and figures and details that marked him as a collector and a connoisseur. She found it attractive, and she knew the power of those feelings herself.

"No," he said, observing the luffing sail. The sail rippled and sagged as the breeze died out and the boat lost much of its speed, so he loosened a knot and tightened a hawser and the rope clicked through the pulley as the boom swung back toward the boat. When the sail filled again with air, they began skidding over the waves.

"You think I'm being pedantic." He tied off the rope with a savage jerk.

Before she could answer he went on, cutting her off with a brisk slice of his hand. "It's all right. Other people have thought that about me, too."

From the way a muscle jumped in his cheek, she could tell he hadn't enjoyed that, and she let him raise the jib without asking any more questions.

To break the silence, she uncorked a bottle of wine.

"Can you drink and drive?" She held up the bottle, and the wind passing over its open neck gave a low hoot.

"Certainly." He looped the rope over the steering wheel again and stepped down into the cabin; though he was invisible, she heard him rattling through drawers. She could see a brown box below a table, with a few odds and ends poking up: screwdrivers and bolt cutters, a length of rope wound into a figure eight, duct tape and fenders, a large pair of camouflage-colored binoculars. Beside the table was a yellow plastic bucket, tied to the table leg, and inside that a square blue sponge.

Soon he emerged with two wineglasses and a stack of paper plates.

"No china?"

"No dishwasher. And I hate a mess."

She poured them both a glass of wine and drank hers quickly. Her second glass she sipped; he hadn't touched his. After she set out the picnic, they ate in comfortable silence, with Steven now and then shifting her from side to side over the food as they tacked into the wind. Close-hauling, he said, returning to the language of the boat, which he obviously enjoyed, and he told her how he was steering by the orange telltales on the sails and mast—little strips of bright plastic ribbon that indicated the wind direction and whether he had his sails correctly rigged to take advantage of it. This time when she made a face at a term— the bitter end of a rope—he explained what he meant and said that before long, the terms would be second nature to her, too.

She put down the wine and sniffed the air.

"That's odd," she said.

"What?"

"It smells like burning coal."

Steven checked the telltales, then told her they were coming about. She ducked as the boom passed, and he congratulated her on her nose.

"That's the power plant on Cape Ann. Coal-burning. It means the wind's from the south now. You'd make a good sailor. I hadn't noticed it yet myself."

They were slicing through the angled, shining faces of the waves, and, farther east, he pointed out becalmed boats that hadn't yet picked up the wind change; she felt exultant.

.   .   .

After a while he said, "You have a nose for smoke."

Her back stiffened; she was sure she knew where the conversation was going.

He kept his eyes level, staring out over the bow and the endless swells. "When the house burned," he said, a quaver in his voice betraying his interest.

She waited but he did not go on. What was it about fire? At the hospital she'd had to stay in afterward, nearly everyone she spoke to seemed to be there because of it. One boy about her age had doused his brother with gasoline while he lay sleeping and then dropped a burning match on him.

"Yes?" she said, bending toward Steven. His interest did not offend her. It was thrilling, in fact, to have him steer her toward once familiar but now generally off-limits conversational territory.

He adjusted the wheel and the boat leaned into the wind, heeling, he called it. She leaned back in counterbalance, flinching when she felt the bruise on her thigh. He was busy, sighting both a buoy and a water tower over a compass, and then drawing on a chart near the wheel.

"I'm taking lines of position," he said, marking down some notes. Then he spoke to her again. "I was going to ask if you were scared."

She tilted her head up to the blue sky, trying to remember. The few clouds seemed very far away, floating on some outer sphere of their own, incapable of affecting her day. "Fear? I suppose I felt that, though I might say more properly that I was terrified." She held a hand to her exposed throat. "And I felt sadness, because despite what my aunt said later, I loved that house."

He was watching her, waiting for her to go on, and she shook off a chill and put her hands under her thighs. "There was a thrill, too. Flying in the face of what was not allowed, Thou shalt not and all that. But mostly I was shocked."

"At what you'd done?"

"Oh no. We both knew we were making the wrong choice, and yet we still made it. What shocked me was the speed. The fire moved very quickly." She pulled her hands free and sat forward, balancing on the edge of the seat. "From the first puff of smoke to smoking embers took just seventeen minutes."

"And your uncle?"

"We didn't know he was there." She finished her wine. Her shoulders were hot from the sun, her hair damp. She remembered the odd sounds the fire had made as it entered the walls, a peculiar sucking noise, and creaking, sounds she'd always imagined to be associated with the hulls of wooden ships and high seas, and here she was on a boat on the water, discussing them for the first time in years. There'd been no mistaking that something disastrous was occurring. For perhaps ten seconds the fire had locked the door in its frame, their lone route of escape, and she'd been convinced she was about to die. Perhaps it had been the same for her uncle.

"It was his own fault. He could have gotten out." Her mother and stepfather had told her that, many times. She looked in her wineglass. A few last drops rocked back and forth up the sides as the boat pushed through the waves, and she held it upside down over the water and let them trail out, her fingers brushing the wave tops. The water was very cold.

"He heard the fire, and the alarms. He went back for things, papers, and his collection of pens. And anyway, he lived for years afterward. It wasn't the fire that killed him. We had meant to set the fire, and for it to burn, but I don't think we quite understood all that would follow."

"Quite a story," Steven said.

"It is, isn't it? One not many can tell, I suppose." She hugged herself.

Steven checked his watch and then made some measurements on the chart.

"What are you doing?"

"Dead reckoning," he said. "It gives us our position." Then

he was hauling down the sails and the boat was slowing. It took him only a minute, the pulleys and metal grommets clinking against the mast as they moved, and when he was done he slipped the rope loop around the steering wheel again. The boat wasn't pushing forward at all now, only bobbing on the waves.

"How about a respite from stories for a tour of the boat?" he said. "Can I show you the cabins?" There was a certain thickness to his voice.

She put her glass down and stood. "I'd love that."

Belowdecks there was a surprisingly wide hallway, yellow light showing across its dark wood from the open cabin doors.

"Port one is made up," he said, and she walked toward it, the door swinging slowly back and forth on oiled hinges. Through the portholes the sun shone in bright circles on the wall, burnishing the mahogany trim, and the room was spare and beautiful: a waist-high bunk with parchment-colored Irish linen sheets and a Hudson Bay blanket, a burled walnut dresser built into the wall with a matching mirror above it, gimballed brass sconces on either side of the mirror. The ceiling was low and cross-beamed and curved above her like a lid.

As she entered the room the boat lurched from a sudden wave, and she stumbled against the bunk; Steven put one hand on her shoulder to steady her and when she leaned close to him he did not retreat. The dark hairs on his arms were standing up, his breathing was fast and shallow, and her own skin was suddenly moist.

She turned into him and squeezed his face between her hands and kissed him, and within seconds, it seemed, her blouse was undone and his head was buried in her chest and his cupped palms were lifting her breasts through the lace of her bra. She arched her back, her throat was curved, her fingers gripped his hair; he used the back of his knuckles on her nipples. Then he was tugging at her shorts and she at his and when hers were around one ankle he grasped her hips and pulled her toward him but she pushed him away and spun around. He bent closer, over her back, and the scent of his cologne was suddenly stronger. His warm mouth moved between her shoulder blades and down the knobs of her spine, and her bruise was throbbing. He traced it with his fingertips and as she opened her legs he thrust into her; she closed her eyes and rose up onto her toes from the force of it and then gripped the raised edge of the bunk and pushed back.

When she opened her eyes her knuckles were white and she could see the swaying of her breasts reflected in the mirror. She could not see Steven's face, just his shoulders and upper arms,

the muscles taut, the veins engorged, and the beautiful mahogany door, swinging to and fro behind him. At last it clicked
shut and she closed her eyes again, wondering how much of their
smooth rolling motion was lust, and how much was dictated by
the sea.

Above decks again, she found the sun inordinately bright.

He rested a hand on her thigh and asked her more about her
past. "You talk," she said, crossing her legs and trapping his
hand. "It's your turn."

He shook his head, and sunlight flashed on his sunglasses.
"My time will come later." He freed his hand. "Right now I
want to know about you."

So she went on. Mostly she talked about Claudia, how close
they'd been, and how hard it was to suddenly be barred from
seeing her, and how soon after the prohibition the fire had been.
For years, she'd been forbidden even to say her cousin's name,
though she'd tracked Claudia through other relatives: her hospitalization and unhappy high school years, her stint at college, her
sudden decision to become a nurse. Jean listed their favorite
games. One had been marbles, which they played after stuffing
themselves with Fudgesicles and soda, and they'd use only blue-

and-white marbles, she remembered, spinning them round and round a copper bowl and staring transfixed at them long after watching had made the two of them become dizzy and sick.

It was something about the interplay of the colors that hooked them, she said, the shifting pattern that you controlled and made anew, second by second. He listened intently, which flattered her; at work her words rarely sparked such attention.

She had to lie down after telling that one: her stomach felt horribly loose. He covered her with a blanket, smoothed down her hair. "Turn your back to the wind," he said. "That will help."

She awoke an hour or two later, with Steven standing beside her, looking out to sea. She stared at him for a few seconds before realizing who he was, where she was. There was a camera around his neck; evidently he'd been taking some pictures. She wondered if he knew he was being watched. He was handsome; his nose ruler-straight.

He glanced down at her and smiled. "Awake?"

She nodded and sat up. Her ribs ached on the side she'd slept on, her clothes felt damp, and they were within sight of shore; the birds were with them again, calling, circling. It was windier now, and colder, and the sun had declined considerably—the boat cast a long shadow on the glittering bronze-colored water.

She couldn't get warm and her mouth tasted horrible, the aftertaste of the Stilton, she decided; what had seemed merely sharp at the time now tasted rotten, and she reached for some wine to rinse it out.

He grabbed her wrist. "That'll be warm. Let me get you something colder. Hold this." He stepped aside from the wheel.

She stood and took it and was immediately surprised at how strongly it tugged against the muscles in her forearms, like something alive.

"See that halyard?" he said, standing behind her and positioning her head so she was looking at the rope rising to the mast. She was aware of the mass of his body at her back, the way it blocked out the wind, and felt her thigh muscles tightening. "That's what you steer by. The lighthouse beyond it? Keep it just to the right of the halyard. The wind will push you toward it, so you have to steer to correct it."

He zipped down to the cabin, sliding the door closed behind him, and returned with a sweating bottle, and she liked his solicitousness; it made up for some of his earlier oddities. He uncorked the wine and poured two glasses and held up his and they clinked them together. She had to put hers down quickly, as the wheel jerked against her single hand and she felt the boat swing away, the sails begin to slacken.

"To a woman who found her sea legs the very first trip," he said, and drank some of his. "That's unusual."

She arched an eyebrow. "Oh? And have there been many others?"

He looked directly at her. "There are always others. But very few are special."

Complimented, she shook out her heavy hair. "I'm surprised I did so well. I take pills for all kinds of things, every allergy in the book. I thought I'd need Dramamine too."

He finished his wine and tucked the glass into a locker. "Ready to handle your first tack?"

She said she was.

"All right," he said. "Remember that it's like backing a car. You steer the wheel in the direction you want to turn."

She nodded.

"And when you're ready, you give the signal, not me. The crew's ready. You'll end up with the bowsprit pointed toward both those stacked rocks and the church steeple rising behind them. That's how you know you're not drifting sideways."

She turned to find where he was pointing.

"All right," she said. "Ready about."

The boat slowed for a moment as it crossed through the wind, then surged forward as the sails filled again. She steered too sharply and a wave broke over their bow, dousing them, but she quickly corrected and within seconds was on course.

"Good," he said, clapping her shoulder, and letting his hand linger. "You'll be a sailor in no time."

They were silent the rest of the short way in, but she didn't mind; it was not an encumbering silence, nor an angry one. Steven reminded her of her father in his emotional coolness, which she preferred, all things considered, to the cloying false friendship of someone like Bonnie, who wished to be her best friend without even knowing her.

He asked her to steer while he prepared the boat for the harbor, untying the boom vang and reefing the sail, putting out the fenders, coiling rope. Always clockwise, she noticed. As they passed the breakwater he said, "If I'd known how much I liked this, I'd have done something to get my own boat much sooner."

"And if I'd known how much I like it," she said, "I'd have sailed before."

He secured the boat and walked her toward her car. Her legs were surprisingly tired, and the first few steps on the dock she found herself bracing for the boards to lurch beneath her, as if it was the land that was treacherous and not the sea, and when they reached the street and he took her hand, it felt natural, though his palm was more callused than it had seemed while moving over her body. She was about to ask him home when he stopped and cleared his throat, and the sound thrilled her, because being with Steven was like being with Claudia had been, only now, as an adult, that sense that someone else was so much like you they might have been your twin. She knew what he was thinking, what was coming, and thought that his place was as good as hers; better even: she could always leave if things went wrong. She shifted the basket hanging from her elbow and leaned close to him.

"Listen," he said. His face was ruddy from the sun, his hair windblown. She pressed his hand to let him know he should ask, and swung the basket behind her, believing he meant to kiss her. In an odd way, she thought, it would be their first kiss: the sex had been so spontaneous that it almost didn't count. She was surprised at her impulsiveness, but not dismayed, the Grieshaber, the sex, it was as if she'd suddenly reinhabited her old self, the person she'd been years before with Claudia, and that pleased her. With him she felt whole again, her again. The connection was deep and palpable and utterly unnecessary to explain.

"I hope you won't think me rude," he said. "But I have a fair amount of work to do cleaning up the boat."

Her knees locked, her breathing clenched, she felt as though she'd been gutted. What was he saying? To her the boat had seemed perfectly clean, but it was clear that he was dismissing her. She let go of his hand and walked on, thinking that perhaps he hadn't enjoyed the sex or the silence after all.

To cover her embarrassment, she was compensatory, overly cool. "No." She folded her arms and watched her feet on the cobbles, taking care not to trip, aware of the bouncing of her breasts beneath her sweater, of the basket bumping at her side. The motion of her breasts struck her as absurd, and it galled her to think he'd seen her naked so shortly before, that even now, her bra was stuffed into the top of the basket. "I understand perfectly," she said. "I've work to do myself."

He was walking beside her, so she quickened her stride and pulled ahead. "I probably shouldn't have come at all."

A loose cobble shifted under her shoe, throwing her off balance, and when he took her arm and stopped she was brought up short and forced to face him.

"Did you not have a good time?" he said.

His directness shocked her into honesty. "Actually, I had a wonderful time."

"Then you shouldn't say that."

She laughed, surprised, and then swallowed the laughter, feeling herself blush, the skin on her face grow tight. What was he about? She pulled her arm away. "I suppose you're right."

He walked beside her to her car and tried once to hold her hand, but she would not allow it, switching the basket so it swung between them. If he'd had a good time, he hadn't said so. She fumbled with her keys. Should she ask him if he had, or should she wait to be invited out again? Perhaps he'd suggest another trip. She put the key in the lock, hoping that he would, since that would be her best chance for revenge, and imagined his mouth clenching into a small bud of disappointment when she refused him.

Before she decided, he opened the door and took her elbow and steered her into the car. The late sun was burning on the windshield, and he blinked his eyes against it.

She moved her legs, gripped the door frame, bent at the waist, and began to slide in, glad her shorts weren't shorter.

"Here you go," he said, and slammed the door on her hand.

The pain was so startling that it was not instantaneous. She saw him shudder, and she had a moment when she was looking at her improperly hinged fingers, knowing the pain was about to come but aware that it was not yet there, and then it enveloped her. It was shattering, so total it seemed akin to the language of pleasure. Her legs went but she would not lean against him, refusing to disintegrate in front of a man who was still largely a stranger, and who caused in her such conflicting emotions; instead, she sagged against the car.

He opened his mouth but no words came out, and his face was as pale as paper, as if he'd never seen the sun. With an effort, she handed him her keys.

"I can't drive," he said. His breathing was very shallow.

She started around for the passenger side, leaning her elbow on the roof for leverage. "I'll shift with my other hand," she said. She needed to get to a hospital quickly; her voice was beginning to shake.

"No." He stopped her. "I mean I can't drive at all."

She tried to comprehend what he was saying, but in her pain the meaning of his words seemed impossible to grasp. He glanced over her shoulder, squeezed her arm, left. Why was he running away? The back of her hand was already purple. Doubling over, she heard a horn.

He'd brought back a taxi; she saw the yellow hood and roof through swimming eyes. She cradled her hand in her lap as she climbed in, fingers curled, palm up, and he stuffed money through the driver's window, gave directions, and banged on the roof; the taxi shot away. She expected bones to burst through her skin, her mouth tasted like old pennies, she bit her tongue to stifle a moan.

Later, she would be angry that he'd not come along, even though she knew people reacted oddly to pain and guilt, but just now, feet jammed against the transmission hump, holding herself rigid in the speeding car, she was grateful not to have to listen to endless apologies. Her agony was pure enough, and she did not want to mix it with anger or disgust.

THE HOSPITAL CORRIDOR WAS TOO BRIGHTLY LIT—THE hanging lights had halos around them—and it smelled of disinfectant, and somewhere farther down it a tinny radio was playing, irritatingly insistent. Jean sat on a bench across from a darkened window, trying not to listen, wondering how blurred people could walk toward her from either end of the corridor without ever seeming to get closer. Their trapped voices echoed and swelled.

She wanted that to stop. Leaning her head back against the polished tiles, she concentrated on her pain, the way it felt round and hollow in her hand, like a memory of pain, a stand-in for the real thing. She'd had enough drugs to ensure that. She stretched out on the bench, which was hard beneath her heels and hips and shoulder blades and head.

"You must lie like that for all eternity." The words were in Claudia's voice, a line from one of their childhood games. Beyond the Divide, the game had been; if you moved even once you were punished. They took turns lying still on a board while watching the other scuttle about, picking roses, pretending to cook, preening before a mirror, all the while secretly mourning, and the thrill was that you got to watch someone crumble at your loss, to see the devastating process of accumulated grief, and all for you. You. Above her, the fluorescent lights buzzed loudly and then softly and then loudly again, following some obscure rhythm that escaped Jean, the light from them throbbing against her closed eyelids as if she were moving beneath them on a stretcher.

When she opened her eyes again, Claudia was standing before her. She had on her white nurse's uniform, and at first Jean didn't recognize her. Jean closed her eyes and counted to five and opened them again and the apparition was still there. She sat up. It was the hair that had thrown her, short now, and permed. Blond. At the wedding it had been black and long.

"It must hurt terribly," Claudia said. She sat beside Jean and took her other hand.

Jean rotated her arm with the heavy cast. Wires were attached to her swollen, discolored fingers, so she could flex them, but she did not try to. The fingers were fat and purple, like rotten sausages. "Not now. It did before, and I think it will again. Can you drive me home?"

"I'm on for another three hours."

"Is that no?"

"Yes."

She leaned back again. Some time passed, though she wasn't sure how much, and then Claudia was standing in front of her once more. She had her hand out, open, and on her palm were three large yellow oblong pills.

"It's Vicodin. I checked your chart. You can have two more safely now, another in two hours."

Jean took them and put all three in her mouth. They were dry at first and she gnawed them, and then they turned bitter, and she was about to ask if she could have something to drink when Claudia said, "Something with a lot of sugar would be best. You'll still be thirsty but your blood won't seem so thick to you, like it's sabotaging your tongue."

It was true; her tongue felt grotesquely swollen, a foreign object stuffed into her mouth and glued there. How had Claudia known?

"I'm a nurse, remember?"

For a while they both were silent and then Claudia was hand-ing her a can of soda, Dr Pepper. They had drunk nothing else for an entire summer. Jean realized she must have slept. Perhaps she needed a room if the drugs were doing this to her, but she wanted to go home, to be surrounded by familiar things. Though it would be weeks before she could take up one of her pens again in that hand, she was sure sorting them would calm her.

She took the soda and sat forward and made an effort to study Claudia. A series of fine white lines, slightly hillocked, marked the webbed skin between her fingers, like a three-dimensional topographical map, scars that Jean herself had, a remnant of their childhood. One of them would turn on a fan and then pull its plug and thrust her fingers through the protective screen as the blades slowed, the object being to see how fast the fan could be going when you stopped it; you lost points if the blades cut you. Still, they didn't allow timing with watches, it was all judgment, and they had both often miscalculated.

"What made you invite me to the wedding?" Jean asked.

"I was filling out the invitation list and the games we used to play just popped into my mind, and I knew I'd never forgive myself if I didn't write you." She squeezed her hand affectionately. "It had been too long, and something about getting married made me miss our games. I wanted to play again."

"When did you do your hair?"

Claudia pushed the tight blond curls up with her palm, looking at herself in the blackened window. "You like?"

Jean dipped her chin in a nod. She was watching the reflection, too.

"Boyd's idea. Our honeymoon starts tomorrow; he wants something different."

"What happened to your eye?" The socket rim was purple and yellow, raised. The slow pulse of a blood vessel showed along its livid curve.

"Boyd's so mad."

"He hit you."

"See? That's just what he says everyone's going to think. A bride on her honeymoon with a black eye. He wanted to put it off even longer, but I said three weeks after the wedding was enough delay."

"Maybe he'll break your hand."

"You weren't honeymooning already, were you?"

"No. But I wasn't expecting to get something broken." Jean inspected the complicated mechanism encasing her hand. "I would've thought I needed at least a second date for that."

"I was going to introduce you. He's always seemed intriguing, if a little odd. I'm sorry if it didn't work out the way you wanted."

Jean shook her head. It gave her the peculiar sensation that her brain was loose and floating, that it was a wet sponge sloshing against the waterlogged casing of her skull, and she took a few seconds before speaking. "Don't be. I didn't mean that. It was an accident, really. Except for the last three minutes the date went well, and I've certainly never had one like it before. He made it memorable." After she said it, she wasn't sure if she meant just the accident, or both that and the sex.

Neither spoke. Jean put her good hand out and stared at the knuckles, so thin compared to the fluid-filled ones of her other hand.

"Promise me one thing."

Claudia nodded.

"You won't tell your mother about this."

"Why not?"

"She'll think we're up to our old tricks again. You know how she blamed me for so much of what happened to us."

After the fire, she had stood beside Claudia on the hill behind the house, skin hot, hair singed, nostrils filled with the sulfurous stink of the smoke, watching the firemen poke with their axes at the glowing rubble, the embers that had once comprised the house. The only things left standing were the three chimneys and the front porch, including its wooden steps and pillars—an entrance to a house no longer there and its hearths. Sally had come toward them, and Jean had slipped away, into the apple orchard with its leaves withered by the intense heat, but for years afterward, she had heard Sally's voice as it came to her that night, repeating over and over again her mantra.

"It was she again, wasn't it? Tell me it wasn't you."

Claudia shifted on the bench beside her. "Yes. The fire upset Mother terribly. A few days after it, she fought with your mother, after Mother had said it was all your fault.

"Your mother was castigating her. 'Everyone got out," she said. 'All you lost were things.'

" 'You don't understand,' Mother said. She was so distraught her face was contorted. Pained. As if she'd been burned in the fire, and not Father. She held both her hands out and I thought she was going to strike her. 'You don't understand,' she said again. ' "Things" are all I have in my life.' "

And they were all gone, of course, Jean thought, the two-hundred-year-old panes of glass, tinted pink because of too much selenide mixed in with the cullet during their manufacture, the daguerreotypes of petty criminals that had lined the stairway wall, the turn-of-the-century celadon tableware.

"Yes," Claudia said. "They were all gone."

A wheeled cart, pushed by a short, balding man in green hospital scrubs, made a racket as it crossed the hallway at a distance. They both tracked its noisy progress until it disappeared.

"So you can see why I don't want her to know," Jean said. "Somehow, this will seem to her a danger to you."

Claudia was back to staring at the black-and-white tile floor, but quite clearly she understood. "All right," she said, sitting straighter. "Though I'm hardly in any danger." Then she added, "He has a lot of accidents."

Jean was silent, thinking of Steven. Two elevator bells dinged farther down the hallway, one after the other. Finally she said, "Mr. Accident."

They both laughed. When they were younger, they had secretly nicknamed people according to their attributes. Mr. Stubble. Miss Cleavage. Mr. Burns.

Jean opened the soda Claudia had brought her and drank half of it, then rested her forehead against the cold, sweating can. "He said he met you here."

"Oh yes. And right from the start I thought of you. He was the man we'd dreamed about when we were younger, but I already had Boyd."

Claudia's pager beeped. She turned it off and stood.

"I'm sorry. I wanted to talk. We didn't get a chance at the

wedding. That whole thing was such a blur." She rested her hand on Jean's shoulder. "Can I call you when I get back?"

Jean nodded. Her tongue was thickening up again, and she had more questions she wanted to ask, but she knew she probably had time for only one or two. "Can I go home?"

"Wait an hour. Then you'll be fine. Or at least your head will be clear, though you might not want it to be."

She pressed down once on Jean's shoulder, firmly, and turned to leave.

"What kind of accidents?"

Claudia gave her a puzzled smile.

"Mr. Accident. Steven." She waved the can at the hallway. "The ones that bring him here."

But Claudia brushed her off. She shook her head and said, "That's not important, really, now that you've met him. Sleep for a little while." She started to walk away. "Then go home."

Three hours later, another nurse shook Jean awake.

"Miss? Are you all right?" she asked.

Jean looked up at the black face bending over her, the features upside down so that the chin appeared like a broad nose, the arc of the pink lips oddly reversed. The woman smelled of vanilla, and for a few seconds Jean was disoriented. Then the muffled paging of a doctor over an intercom—that old, familiar sound—made her realize she was still in the hospital; perhaps she'd been dreaming.

"Did Claudia ask you to check?"

"Sorry?"

"Never mind." Jean wiped drool from her cheek, raised herself to a sitting position, and stood. She swayed on her feet and her head spun. Her stomach was hollow and her legs grew heavier, as if they were a pair of waders and water was flooding into them.

The nurse was holding a can of Dr Pepper in one palm, label out, as if displaying it for an ad. Jean thought it was probably hers, and that the nurse was cleaning up after her, but then the nurse raised it to her lips and took a long swallow.

"I'm fine," Jean said. "Thank you. I can make it now."

The nurse went away and Jean listened to her padded footsteps disappearing behind her, then focused on her own feet, willing them to move. Her eye sockets seemed to have grown and her eyeballs felt crisp and skeletal within them; her mouth was horribly dry. She took a step, then another, and it was as though her head was filling with helium. She walked down the hall toward the exit, pressing her good hand against the cool yellow tiles every other step for support.

. . .

Jean sat in the kitchen, which smelled of lemons and coffee, wondering what to do. She was warming herself in the morning sun, the breakfast dishes pushed aside, thinking of Steven. In six days, he had neither called nor returned her car, though she'd found a dozen long-stemmed roses waiting for her inside the building doorway when she'd come home from the hospital, and upstairs in her apartment the message light on her answering machine had been blinking. But she was allergic to roses—as soon as she smelled them her eyes watered and her nose started to run and her throat swelled painfully—and she'd kicked them out into the alley for someone else to take, shredding the card without reading it, and later, upstairs, had deleted her messages without listening to them, sure that a couple, at least, were from him. She'd been in no mood for an apology and the roses had only heightened her anger, but now she regretted her response, finding it both ill-conceived and hasty.

Steven wasn't one to apologize; he'd probably wanted to set up a way to return her car. Still, he should have called again; that he hadn't, bothered her. She swept the dishes toward her with the cast, then stood and put them in the sink.

On the counter was the latest missive from her neighbor, Mrs. Olsen, an article concerning a woman who'd been beaten so badly she'd ended up comatose in the hospital, and who was not expected to recover. No one knew who she was: she'd been found in the Fens without identification and didn't match any missing persons' descriptions. She was about thirty, she was tall, she had red hair, she was wearing blue Lycra pants and a Babson College sweatshirt, she had two shoes but the shoes were not a pair and were on the wrong feet. Mrs. Olsen had underlined all these details.

She'd heard Jean sneezing and coughing in the alley the night she came back from the hospital, and had let her in and given her the spare apartment key she kept for her, but she'd been perturbed by the cast and by Jean's swollen fingers.

"What happened to you?" she'd asked, holding the key close to her until Jean answered.

"An accident," Jean had said, not wanting to discuss it.

"What kind of accident breaks your hand?"

"A painful one."

"Well, it must've been. Your hand looks terrible. *You* look terrible."

"Why, thank you. So kind of you to notice."

"Nothing to be kind about. It's the truth."

She offered Jean tea—a first—in the hope that Jean would become loquacious while drinking it, and Jean had initially declined, but when Mrs. Olsen pressed her, Jean relented: her eyes were still leaking and the back of her throat felt raw, as though she'd run a file down it, and tea sounded soothing, but she hadn't the energy to fix it herself.

The apartment, dim and cluttered and smelling of naphtha, was laid out exactly like her own. Mrs. Olsen shuffled in ahead of her, Jean hoping that conversation with someone familiar, however much a stranger, might not be a bad thing; she wouldn't have to think about what had happened. Mrs. Olsen stopped halfway down the hall and took a lightbulb from a table.

"Put this in for me, will you?" she said, pulling out a chair. "I'll fall if I stand up on this."

After Jean mounted the chair and screwed the bulb into the sconce, she tried the switch, but even then the light didn't work. Mrs. Olsen seemed not to notice. They continued on to the kitchen, where the overhead light turned the plastic-coated windows opaque and where the smell of naphtha seemed more concentrated; Mrs. Olsen had Jean sit at the table, a square red linoleum affair edged in nickel, and wouldn't let her help.

"No, no," she said, getting out a mug and pouring it half full of milk without asking Jean if she took any in her tea. "Sit. You need to rest. I'll take care of you."

When the water boiled—the kettle whistling for a few sec-

onds before she noticed it—Mrs. Olsen filled Jean's cup and un-
wrapped graham crackers from three layers of plastic and wax
paper, gave one to Jean, rewrapped them, and returned them to
their tin. She pressed her fingertips to the crumbs that had fallen
on the counter and licked them, then sat across from Jean and
began to talk.

She'd had a son, but he'd died years ago, in New York City,
Johnny, a good boy, she said, he'd been working down there, he
had a good job. She took down his picture from the wall—he
was an overweight boy with shaggy hair and small eyes and
a thin mustache—and gave it to Jean to look at, and when
Jean had studied it long enough Mrs. Olsen took it back and
rehung it and then went on with her story. Johnny had been
murdered in his own apartment, and since then Mrs. Olsen had
been alone. She'd also had a husband, she said, but he'd been
gone so long she no longer remembered him. His picture she
merely pointed out.

Jean realized she'd been brought in to listen, so while Mrs.
Olsen talked, she observed her, the yellow streaks in her ponytailed white hair, the too-big false teeth, which looked alarm-
ingly ready to fall out, the bony hands. Then her attention
shifted to the kitchen, the greasy olive-green oven, the cabinet
doors that didn't shut, the faux brick rising halfway up the open

wall with the last course topped by faux mortar. It was like her own kitchen—she even had the same three-tiered metal fruit basket hanging from the dropped ceiling—just older and dirtier and out of style, and in her altered state, Jean could all too easily imagine herself hurtling through time to end up like this, so old she was ancient, licking crumbs from her fingers and dragooning some stranger into listening to her long tale of woe, which would differ only in stray details, not in import, from Mrs. Olsen's. *I met a man once, who I thought was the one, but all he did was break my fingers.* An odd image of Mrs. Olsen's soul struggling to escape her bony, painful body came to mind, and in the middle of one of Mrs. Olsen's sentences, Jean stood and said she had to leave.

Mrs. Olsen ducked her head. "You don't have to go yet. Sit."

"No, I really do. It's been a long day, and one I'd just as soon have end. Please." She put her cast to her chest and held out her good hand. "The key."

Mrs. Olsen had given it up, reluctantly, and seemed to have avoided Jean thereafter, but the article showed that the old woman, far from forgetting her, was instead intensifying her efforts to warn Jean about the perils loose in the world. Three times in the past four days she'd clipped pieces from the *Herald* about women who'd been beaten or robbed or raped, and sent them up to Jean, heavily underlined but with the green crayon messages that normally accompanied them noticeably absent. Jean, no doubt, was meant to draw conclusions about parallels to her own situation by herself. She looked this one over once more, then crumpled it and threw it away.

From the refrigerator she took a nearly empty bottle of red wine and poured herself the last glass. The wine was chilled, slightly tannic, and she drank it while searching through the phone book. She didn't find Steven's name, and directory assistance had no listing for him, and Claudia was still away on her honeymoon. But even if she waited a week for Claudia's return, it might still be impossible to contact Steven by phone, so she decided that the only thing to do was to go and get the keys and the car herself.

She almost admired that Steven could play hard to get in the wake of what had happened, an accident, certainly, but nonetheless his fault, and yet by forcing her to come to him he made it seem that *he* was the one who had been wronged, not she. She meant to tell him that when she saw him and would be happy to do so, since she felt herself immune to his charms now. Hearing her, he would get his hopes up, and then she would take her keys and drive away, ignoring his protests. By hooking the cast around the gear shift, she would be able to manage it herself.

She closed the phone book and put aside the wine and took up her purse and left.

On the stairs, she heard Mrs. Olsen's slippers scraping over the linoleum in the hallway, like sandpaper over wood. She was coming to watch Jean leave, and the thought of her boxed up in that dim hallway behind her closed door, spending her days listening to the comings and goings of her neighbors while peering through the peephole at the back of their heads, depressed Jean immeasurably. What a grim, pointless existence, she thought, as she quickened her pace down the stairs, made worse by the fact that there were probably countless others like her in buildings all over the city, old women hanging on to life by eavesdropping on the lives of others. She resented being made a part of it.

Outside, as she turned out of her alley onto Newberry Street and emerged into a burst of green, she found her depression deepening. The trees were in full leaf at last and the morning sunlight clipped the tops of buildings and then filtered down through the overhanging branches, picking up the cast of their color in its fall, and the street was noisy and crowded. Awnings had been rolled down, shop doors were propped open with crates of grapefruit and racks of clothes, and swarms of people streamed in and out of the stores, arms filled with packages, which was exactly what she would expect for a Saturday morning. But all the activity seemed calculated to dismay her, to remind her that the journey on which she was about to embark had ended in disaster not even a week before. At the next corner was a taxi. She tucked her purse under her arm and hurried after it.

The cab ride cost thirty dollars. Her car was where she'd left it, parked flush against the high brick curb on a curving side street, but in only six days it had taken on the look of an abandoned vehicle. A stack of fluorescent orange parking tickets flapped under the windshield wipers, salt spray had dulled the finish, cigarette butts and scraps of paper were blown against the tires. She paid the driver, a Croatian with lank hair and clothes that smelled like they'd been stored in a smokehouse, and stepped out.

The car was locked, which didn't surprise her, though she'd hoped Steven might have left it open and tucked the keys under the driver's seat, since she had no extras, and now she would have to ask for their return. She headed toward the docks, her clogs knocking on the cobbles.

Steven's boat was bobbing in its slip, and the sight of it calmed her. Many of the other slips were empty, which was just as well, she thought; she had enough nosy people in her life and she didn't want the woman in the saffron-yellow pantsuit bothering her again. Her boat, the *Lucky Lady,* was one of the ones that was gone.

The stairs down from street level smelled of tar, and when she reached the bottom she slowed her pace; the dock planking gave unevenly beneath her clogs and she was afraid of stumbling. Her footsteps echoed over the water and at the sound of them a single gull, floating in an empty anchorage, flapped its wings, lifted off the water, and flew away into the endless blue sky. She wished she hadn't forgotten her sunglasses.

The boat seemed deserted. She stood beside it and called out to Steven, and then again, louder, when she got no answer. She waited, listening, before calling a third time. Two crows flew overhead, bickering, a bell buoy rang, wood squeaked against rubber, and then, while she was waiting, something flashing in the sun caught her eye: her keys, she realized, swaying as the boat moved, dangling from the taffrail on a length of twine. She put her purse down, because she would have to stretch to reach them.

She leaned forward awkwardly when the boat rose toward her, and as her center of gravity tipped out over water she felt herself beginning to fall—she had a brief mental image of being crushed between the boat and the dock—and then she grabbed for the rail as it moved away from her, gripped it, and held on. Her feet lifted clear of the dock and her cast banged against the hull, sending a sharp pain through her hand, and then her clogs slipped off her feet and splashed into the water and sank. For a few seconds she dangled in space by her one good hand.

The skin on her palm began to get slick; she felt her grip slipping but just then the boat rolled back and she grabbed the keys and dropped onto the dock; once she had her balance she reached out and tried to kick the hull. Her cast made the boat hard to reach. She had to lean back against its weight, which shortened her stride, and she ended up kicking at air, which only made her angrier. Spinning around to search the dock for something to throw, she was startled to find herself face to face with a man who'd evidently been watching her. He was standing by a pile of lobster traps with an absolutely neutral expression on his face, unremarkable-looking except for his bushy beard and his pink skin, the color of boiled shrimp.

"Going to buy her?" He nodded at the boat without taking his eyes off Jean. The sleeves of his plaid shirt were cut off, and even the skin on his arms was pink.

"No." She shivered and smoothed her dress with her cast, convinced he'd seen more of her than she'd have liked. Even now, watching her, he seemed to be picturing her hanging from the rising rail, hem sliding up the back of her thighs. She took a step backward, knelt to pick up her purse, and made an effort to control her breathing. "I was looking for the owner."

"Too late." He'd begun to sweat. Suddenly and all at once, his forehead was beaded with perspiration, like a glass removed from refrigeration.

"I know." She let out a long sigh. Her hand hurt, and she seemed to have wrenched her back. "I called out but no one answered."

"She's gone," he said, jerking a thumb skyward.

"She?" Jean said.

He ignored her question and climbed down a ladder to a skiff and started its outboard. The smell of gas came to her sharply. He tinkered with the throttle as she stood at the top of the ladder, hoping to catch his attention, but he untied from the piling and pushed off and steered the boat around the curve of the breakwater without once looking back. From there he turned due east and headed out beyond a point of rocks, trailing a cloud of blue smoke, and as the sound of his engine died out and the smoke dissipated and his wake disappeared, the harbor grew as still as a painting.

She was unsure what to make of him. He was odd, certainly, even creepy, and she told herself that she'd probably misunderstood him. She looked at Steven's boat again, but she'd lost the desire to strike it, so she tried to locate her clogs in the water instead. The angle of the sun turned the harbor's surface opaque and she could see nothing beyond her own wavering reflection overlapping that of the boat, and she watched the boat's blue hull slide back and forth under her own image until she began to feel dizzy, when she decided she had no other course than to head home. She wasn't about to go into the oily water after the clogs.

As she started back up the dock, the smell of gas was replaced by the smell of tar, and she told herself that perhaps the trip had been a success after all, despite the pain in her back and hand, the loss of her clogs, and the lack of a chance to tell off Steven. She had her keys, she would have her car.

But the walk to the car made her drop that pretense. By the time she reached it, she was hobbling on two cut feet, her toes and heels were blackened with tar, and she found herself regretting the missed opportunity to tell Steven exactly what she thought of him. Did he believe she was the kind of woman he could screw and forget? More than anything, she realized, she wanted another chance to see him, a last face-to-face meeting, where she could have the final word.

THE PETTIGREW ADS NEEDED TWEAKING. BONNIE SAID their executives were a little unhappy with the comps, and though it was Monday morning—normally not the best time for creative work—Bonnie had taken off the previous week, and now Pettigrew wanted a rush job.

"A *little* unhappy?" Jean said. They were in Bonnie's office. "What does that mean?"

Jean hadn't had enough coffee yet; her head ached, and the smell of patchouli didn't help. Bonnie had so much on that Jean suspected she'd rolled in it. In the background, she heard one of the holistic relaxation tapes Bonnie favored: birds singing, and running water, which always made Jean feel like she had to go to the bathroom. This one, with its endless scroll of breaking waves, was even worse, as it reminded her of the fiasco at the dock.

"Sorry," Bonnie said, and shrugged. She was sitting at her drafting table, spinning the returned package beneath her finger. "They didn't give us more to go on."

She studied Jean as Jean took the package from her, and finally she said, "You look different."

Jean held up her arm. "It's the cast. A new fashion accessory."

"Not that. Your hair. It's quite a change."

"You don't like it."

"I didn't say that."

"You didn't say you did."

"Well," Bonnie said, flushing, "let's leave the semantic games for later," and Jean knew she'd been right.

It didn't bother her; she'd never sought Bonnie's approval and if she'd earned it this time, she probably would have been disappointed; still, she checked her reflection in Bonnie's window, touching the new cut with the cast. She looked good blond.

"Yes, you do," Bonnie said.

Evidently, Jean had spoken aloud. She sorted through the proofs. They were bright, glossy, dramatic; it did not surprise her that Pettigrew was unhappy with them. She'd become disenchanted with the campaign herself, though she'd created it, just over a year before, a series of ads featuring two constants—a plea and an ugly man—and two variables, the Pettigrew mirrors and a slew of simple tags, all of which were variations on a theme.

What we put into it is often more beautiful than what you do.

Upon reflection, we rarely get back what we put into it.

When you look at us, you see yourself. Unfortunately, so do we.

The mirrors varied, too: some were tall and elegant, others smaller with sophisticated, intricate frames, but they were all featured in spectacular locales: a boulder-strewn terrace above a heaving sea, a tiled patio surrounded by lush tropical growth, poolside in the middle of a vast desert plain. Sometimes the man standing before them wore a white towel around his waist, but for the full-length mirrors he was naked, inspecting his swollen belly and dimpled, baggy skin from the side. The plea always ran at the bottom.

Please. Buy us only if you should.

The ads had created a minor stir in the advertising world, and had been the occasion of a loud and protracted argument between Jean and Bonnie just after Bonnie was hired. At that point the ads were still in the planning stage.

Bonnie had walked into Jean's office and spread the dummies on her desk and begun with no preliminaries.

"These are insulting."

"Yes. Rather. That's the point." Jean had thought that obvious; she was a little offended at having to explain it. She sat back and waited for more, resisting the temptation to retch at the smell of patchouli.

"They'll be disastrous," Bonnie said.

"On the contrary; they'll be wildly successful. Exclusivity— the chance to be truly unique—is seductive."

She knew whereof she spoke. Her first hit campaign had been based on exclusivity, for a perfume. *Not for everybody,* read the tag. *Probably not even for you.* For three months the client ran just the copy in women's magazines, only the words without any visual, and with nothing to indicate what the ad was about; by the time the tag finally appeared over the bottled perfume, it was already the subject of much speculation. The perfume itself, launched shortly thereafter, had been an instant success, though Jean herself thought it smelled of Clorox.

Once she'd bought a couch, ormolu and distressed leather, turned spindle legs, a slight, slanted curve to the back; she'd never seen anything like it. Though it was twice as expensive as everything else she'd looked at, she bought it on the spot, and she'd loved it, its lines, its smell, its supple leather against her bare skin. A month later she'd been taken into a furniture ware-house by a buyer and seen towering stacks of the same couch awaiting their cushions and upholstery, and her own purchase felt incontrovertibly reduced. She'd known abstractly of course that others would buy similar couches, but seeing them so obviously mass-produced had ruined her illusions of singularity, and she rarely sat on it now, she never bent to smell its leather. If she'd seen the stacked couches first, she'd never have bought one.

"Violently insisted upon, exclusivity is even more of a draw," she said to Bonnie. "Women who see the ads for these mirrors will think the insults are aimed at everyone else."

"You're suggesting that these will work for every reader?"

"For the discerning ones, the ones we're after. Look." She leaned over the dummies. "Pettigrew isn't moving a million units a year as it is, they simply want a greater proportion of those about to buy. And everyone wants to think they're special, or original, or peculiar."

"Peculiar?"

From her expression, Jean knew Bonnie was thinking about Jean's past, the rumors of extensive therapy and a long hospitalization, the outbursts she'd been prone to before taking a six-month medical leave. It was all in her files.

"Peculiar," she repeated, not bothering to hide her irritation. "In the sense of not like others, exclusively one's own."

Bonnie fell silent, as if she was thinking, but Jean could tell she was already convinced; her voice had been steadily losing its edge. Still, there was a protocol to these things. Bonnie was the new boss, she would not go down without scoring points. She shuffled through the mock-ups.

"Then we can't have a woman as the model. It has to be a man."

Jean was about to protest, but Bonnie held up a finger to forestall her.

"Women buy 80 percent of furniture."

"I know that. The ads are aimed at women."

"Then we can't risk offending any of our potential buyers." Bonnie straightened the file and closed it. "Small as that pool will be."

Jean had argued vociferously—others artists heard her, even came into her office the next day to comment on it—but Bonnie refused to waver, and finally Jean relented. Secretly, she thought Bonnie wanted a man in the ad because the female model looked too much like an older version of Bonnie herself, the same poodly hair, the same pointy chin, the same pinched features, yet the similarities had been accidental; Jean had chosen the model because she reminded her of her Aunt Sally.

The ads had worked, despite Bonnie's misgivings. Some customers were angry; they wrote letters saying they were offended, but Jean pointed out that it meant they remembered the Pettigrew name, and, more important, after only two months sales spiked noticeably. Now, however, Jean thought the ads were getting stale, and perhaps that's what the Pettigrew executives were reacting to, even without knowing it. It irked her that the Pettigrew people were smart enough to intuit the need for a change before she herself had. She rested the dummies against her cast.

"Perhaps the whole concept should go."

"But the campaign's so successful," Bonnie said.

"Precisely."

"And you want to scrap it? Are you nuts?"

"My sanity isn't the issue. The campaign is, and it's getting *too* successful. That will backfire soon; everyone will tire of it. We need to change it, take off from it, before that happens."

"How?"

Jean shifted. The cast made her shoulder uncomfortable if she stood too long in one position, and her back was still sore. "I don't know. I just know we don't want to let it get old for others. By then, it will be too late; we'll have to abandon the campaign entirely."

"Well, when you come up with a variation, let me know. Until then, we go with it as it is."

"Fine." She moved closer to Bonnie's chair, despite the patchouli, wanting to get on with it. She could see that it would always be like this, month after month, year after year—she would have to fight with Bonnie to get her to understand what should have been perfectly obvious. It was a depressing prospect.

Bonnie began drawing on a sheet of blank paper, ghosting the ad.

"Start in the upper left corner."

"Why?"

"Because it's my account."

"I'm drawing it."

"And my name's on it. I want it done my way."

"Jean."

"I need to see it take form, and that's where I always start."

Bonnie put down her pencil and sighed, which meant she'd indulge her. She rubbed her eyes with her thumbs and then began again, with a fresh piece of paper. The ad appeared slowly.

"That's it," Jean said, nodding. "Your letters are better that way, simpler." She had to admit they were neater than her own, that Bonnie was the superior calligrapher. Still, something was missing from the work, some precise, subtle change which would give the ad the necessary new flair, and she was certain that even if Bonnie worked on the ad for months, she wouldn't unearth it.

She watched Bonnie's pencil move, the short, hatched strokes, and waited for inspiration. It certainly wouldn't come from Bonnie's office, jammed as it was with macramé plant hangers and Victorian candle tables and heavy oak furniture. In an open desk drawer, the bottom left one, where Jean herself kept a bottle of Calvados and a hand-blocked silk scarf, were several opened boxes of Rice Krispies Treats and layer after layer of packages of Brach's candy. Which was fitting. Jean had often thought that if Bonnie had a spirit, it would be cluttered and received, prepackaged. She had to remind herself to stay focused on the work.

After fifteen minutes, Bonnie stopped to stretch her back. She tilted her head and looked at what she'd done from a different perspective. Satisfied, she smiled.

"You were right. Starting that way helps define it somehow."

Jean cleared her throat; she didn't see it, but she would not voice her doubts until she had a solution. In the background, she heard the tape with its endlessly breaking waves.

Bonnie laid the pencils aside and snapped the paper free from the sheets beneath it, holding it away from her and turning it upside down to study the relationships of its forms, an old artist's trick. "I'm sorry your date last week was such a dead-dogger," she said. "You seemed to be looking forward to it."

Jean bristled. Why did Bonnie think that working together gave her license to pry? In this way, too, she reminded Jean of her aunt Sally, stirring up trouble where she didn't belong.

"The date was fine. It's car doors that are the problem. I'd go out with him again in a minute," she said, surprising even herself with her defense of a man who'd smashed her fingers and then left her car keys dangling from the rail of a boat. But at least he'd not thought it his right to comment upon her life.

She reached over Bonnie's shoulder for the paper and put it back on the table, smudging out some of the letters with her thumb. "It's still not there yet," she said. "We need to do better. Try again."

She took her time walking home after work, detouring to go by the waterfront, seeking relief from the hot, still air. In Christopher Columbus park, where she'd once witnessed a fistfight between two men during a saint's festival—maroon drops of blood spinning from one man's squashed nose and spotting the gray paving stones—she sat on a bench and watched ferries cross the harbor, white against the blue water. The park was surprisingly empty. A seagull strutted back and forth in front of her, pecking at cigarette butts and bottle caps caught between the pavers, and after half an hour a breeze came up; the water began to stir, smelling alternately briny and rotten, and small waves lapped at the shore.

Just after the Custom House clock sounded the hour, a tender wound through the anchored boats toward the seawall. The blue light at its bow disappeared from sight, then the boat itself did, and then its engine cut, leaving only the sound of wavelets sloshing against its sides. Seconds later, a woman wearing a black evening dress and heels climbed into view on a ladder Jean had never known was there.

She paused at the top of the ladder, gave Jean the briefest of smiles, checked her hair in a compact, and walked away, picking her feet up so far on each stride that Jean could see the tan bottoms of her shoes. When she turned a corner, Jean took it as a sign that she should go home, too.

Once there, she uncorked a bottle of chilled white wine and poured herself the largest glass she could find, a brandy snifter Oliver Brisbane had given her years before. That the glass was dusty didn't bother her. It was almost like drinking from a bowl. When she put the corkscrew away she found Steven's letter containing his directions, and held it in her lap, trying to decide whether to simply burn it or to tear it into pieces first, and then to burn it.

She drank one glass, then another, and a drop of condensation slid from the glass onto the envelope, landing on her name, which dissolved into a runny blue blur. The pang of grief she felt at this startled her into taking the letter out and spreading it open on the table, where she was careful not to touch the ink, lest more of it begin to run. She noticed again Steven's beautiful hand and wished that her own were more like it.

There was still some light in the sky. From a kitchen drawer she got out several sheets of onionskin, and from her pen cabinet she took the Grieshaber. Carefully, she placed a sheet of onionskin over the first page of the letter, weighting it with her cast so that the thin paper would not slip or tear, and began to trace his letter, word for word, the square upright *U*'s, the fluid *S*'s, the break before all the *T*'s. *Turn right out of your alley onto Newberry Street and then left on Clarendon Street,* she began, and continued on to the end.

Copying the entire letter took half an hour; she had to stop several times to straighten her fingers, keeping them from cramping, but she worked quickly nonetheless, against the fading light, and when she was done she was happy for once with her own handwriting, finding at the end of the process that the invitation had become her own as much as his. The letter was like his, of course, but changed enough to be something new; she could see a slight difference in the arc of the loops and in the pressure of her punctuation, and the ink was different, black rather than blue.

Done, she folded hers away and threw out his, after tearing it into neat squares. She debated with herself what to do with the envelope, for it seemed ruined by the smear of her name, but as she had none that were similar, she decided in the end to reuse it. After putting the envelope and her pen back in their places, she finished off the wine and sat at the table until the last light disappeared from high up on her apartment walls, when she readied herself for bed.

Folding back the covers, she felt the dull ache of hunger deep in her stomach—she had not eaten since lunch—but she ignored it and climbed into bed, thinking ahead, knowing that she would take herself up on the invitation, and that, sometime soon, she would see Steven again.

THE BUS'S HYDRAULIC DOOR SIGHED AND SWIVELED SHUT behind Jean, the engine revved, the bus moved off. She did not mind the rank diesel cloud ascending in its wake; what distressed her were the parked cars jamming the streets into town, windshields flaming in the morning sun—the market had never been so crowded. She stood on the blacktop, reflected heat rising around her ankles and calves, and told herself to ignore the crowd and to concentrate on what she had come for. She would not be lucky enough to find another Grieshaber, she knew, but even a smaller triumph would be worthwhile. In hopes of it, she'd switched perfumes again, back to *Fracas*. After all, the last time she'd worn it, she'd met Steven.

Shifting her bag to the hand with the cast, she started off. People swarmed around the booths and tables and down the twisting side streets, surrounding Jean with surging voices and a confusing mixture of perfumes and colognes, and when they pushed against her she had to restrain herself from using her elbows or swinging the cast to get by. She knew it was unhealthy to feel this way, but she couldn't help it; she was continually startled by the volume of the noise and the density of the crowd, as if she'd gone to the desert for solitude and found the isolated cave she'd chosen packed with the boisterous occupants of a tour bus. Outside the café was a line, tanned men and women wearing khakis or plaid skirts and polo shirts, not the normal customers, and the reason for the change was simple—the paper's weekend supplement contained an article trumpeting the flea market as a great unknown Sunday getaway within easy reach of the city. That the weather was particularly fine hadn't helped, as even the most sluggardly city resident seemed to have been roused by the blue skies and warm day to descend upon the fair.

The woman with the melted sugar dogs was gone, replaced by another woman, who had racks of appliquéd polyester sweatshirts hanging above her as she crocheted, ugly, bright colors, common designs; they were nothing Jean wanted. The farmer at the next table still had his cigar box, but it was filled now with bills and coins, which disappointed her. He might not have recognized her as a short-haired blond, and if he'd restocked his supply, she felt she might have bested him once again.

At one stall she bought a forest-green Eversharp Skyline,

gold-banded with a gold-filled cap and nib, a bargain at twenty-five dollars, and toward the waterfront she discovered three pens in a junk bin. Two were identical pearl-gray Salz Brothers, probably from the fifties, the third a blue-speckled Conklin, which had a strand of red yarn wrapped around it, knotted under the pocket clip. She had no interest in the Salz Brothers—she had that model already—but she removed the yarn and held the Conklin up to the light, twirling it, and the speckles glinted, the sign of authenticity.

Next to her stood a couple, about her age, watching what she did. She could not see their eyes behind their sunglasses, only her own reflection, but the man's forehead was sweating; perhaps he was bothered by the heat. Jean unscrewed the cap and looked inside—a string of numbers was stamped around the circumference, ending in 35, and any of the 1930s series was worth at least a hundred and fifty dollars, possibly two hundred, to the right buyer. Partially, that depended on the nib, whether it had been used often enough to write itself to someone else's hand—the angle one habitually wrote at—or if it still had the chance to be broken in. She uncapped the pen and experimented with it, writing on a scratch pad at various angles, seeking ones that skipped and were therefore wrong, but her left hand lacked the proper sensitivity to detect the ghost of another's working against the motions of her own.

When she asked the price, the vendor, whom she had bought from before, said, "One hundred and sixty-five dollars," without looking up from her magazine. She was reading a quiz, her strawberry-blond bangs hanging down over her eyes. *"Does Your Man Really Love You? A Dozen Answers in as Many Minutes Will Tell You the Truth."* It took Jean a few seconds to decipher the title, reading it upside down.

One sixty-five was a trifle high, given her uncertainty about the nib, but Jean didn't have the spirit to haggle today, and not doing so might incline the vendor to deal on another occasion: she wouldn't see Jean as grasping or unreasonable. The language of bargaining, which was the key to collecting, was mostly unspoken, based on feeling and perception, and this was a time to put quietness to her own uses.

"Fair enough," she said, and paid without quibbling.

As she got her change, the man who had been watching Jean unscrewed the cap of one of the Salz Brothers pens and began inspecting it, though Jean knew he'd find nothing there. Salz Brothers, like Omas, had never inscribed the insides of their caps—for them, all that mattered was the glittering surface.

Then he wrote with the pen on the back of his forefinger, nodded, seemingly satisfied, caught his wife's eye, and asked the vendor the price of the pen.

She marked her place in the magazine with a metal ruler and stood with an effort, pushing off the table with both fists, then propelled herself along by leaning forward and sliding her immobile legs a few feet to the side over the pavement, and then moving her meaty fists and repeating the process once again. At the edge of the table, on a pile of plastic-wrapped vintage seed catalogs, was a fat, ravaged *Plummerman's Antiques* and after flipping through several pages, she made a show of closing the book and waving her hands. "It's too nice a day for this," she said, sliding back toward her seat. "I won't charge you their price. Sixty-five seems right."

The man whispered something to his wife, who whispered back, and both looked at Jean, searching for clues. The woman was small and mousy, her thin hair very straight. Jean smiled.

"Sixty-three," the man said, still watching Jean.

The vendor sighed, shook her head, then let her shoulders sag. "All right," she said at last, holding out a plump, red hand. "Take advantage of me. See if I care."

The man smiled at her performance. "That's a fair deal all the way around."

His wife worked three twenties from her wallet and handed them over, and he added three creased singles.

Before they left, Jean pulled a twenty from her purse and put it on the table, within the vendor's reach. "Here," she said, taking the other Salz Brothers pen. "You can keep the change."

The vendor's cheeks reddened and she opened her mouth to protest, but she couldn't keep up the front and bent over laughing, her stomach heaving with delight. The man and the woman turned abruptly and shouldered through the crowd, obviously offended, but Jean felt no pity for them. If one didn't speak the language, one had no business being involved, and she was not about to reveal its secrets to the uninitiated. Besides, if their interest was genuine, they would discover them anyway on their own, as she herself had done, slowly, with much effort, and over a great amount of time. Years from now, they might look back and count today as step one.

In the shade of a beech tree, where the air was cooler and smelled mossy, she set out her lunch on a stone wall: roasted red peppers, feta, and olive oil on ciabatta, a shredded carrot and cucumber salad, marinated artichoke hearts, plums, a thermos of black Russian iced tea. She used the white paper bag the bread had come in as a placemat, and when she unscrewed the thermos top, the tea was so cold it smoked. On her lap she spread her copy of the invitation, and looking at it, she began to retrace her morning.

The neighborhood streets had been early-Sunday-morning empty. The milky blue light, the parked cars, the absence of sounds and smells; she could be lifted from a deep sleep and put down there any time of the year and know what month it was, what day of the week, even probably what hour, simply by the light and noise. That familiarity usually made her happy, but this morning it had felt constricting. A thin, glowing layer of salt covered the butcher blocks in the meat market, as if they'd been frosted, and the stores' plate-glass windows shone, and she'd avoided watching her reflection ripple across them.

The Common had been too quiet, Government Center vast and deserted except for a flock of gulls, the birds standing on the brick plaza as if in formation, heads lowered into their bodies, eyes closed, all of them facing east. Many appeared to have only one leg. Her footsteps—loud, echoing, and without voices to drown them out sounding somehow invasive—stirred them up like wind over wheat, and they spread their wings and wobbled toward her and began to caw. As she passed through them, their feathers brushed against her skin.

At Haymarket, she'd boarded the North Shore bus, the only

passenger, and sat far enough away from the driver that she wouldn't have to talk, and as the bus rose up the access ramp to the Tobin Bridge and crossed over the black and seemingly still Mystic River, she felt the engine's vibrations in her back and thighs. Almost immediately, the bus's route began to diverge from the one she'd written out, and now, as she began jotting down the differences in the margins of the letter—detouring through Lynn instead of bypassing it, winding away from the sea at every chance instead of veering toward it, disembarking at the edge of town instead of by the water—two overweight, middle-aged women approached her.

"Excuse me, Miss," the shorter one said. She was holding an insulated coffee cup, dark lipstick smearing its rim. "We couldn't help noticing your lunch. Could you tell us where in town you bought it?"

"I'm afraid not," Jean said. She folded away her letter and tucked it back in her purse. "I put it together myself."

"But surely you bought it here, the ingredients."

"There isn't anyplace in town that sells these things."

The woman watched Jean, as if expecting her to say she was joking, and then turned to her companion, a redhead. "Friendly locals, aren't they?" she said.

"Yes," the other one said. She was wearing sensible shoes and creased jeans; her stomach bulged above them. If she were younger, Jean would have suspected she was pregnant. "The article didn't mention anything about that, though."

They had taken her for a local because she was sitting on a stone wall that ran beside a driveway, Jean understood that, and she thought of setting them straight, of protesting that she was simply being honest, that it was true, that the town was not a good one for food. But just as she was about to speak she saw Steven halfway up the street, and it surprised her so that she stood, which the women mistook for aggression. The redhead raised her paper for protection and her friend backed away, yelping as hot coffee splashed over her wrist.

They muttered something as they left about Jean being a bitch, but she barely heard them; for her, they existed only as a nuisance. Steven seemed to be discussing a particular object with a vendor, he had it in his hands, and then he turned in her direction and held it to his face. Binoculars; the lenses flashed in the sun. He was looking beyond her to the sea, adjusting the focus to observe something more closely, and, swiveling to find what he might be studying, she saw a string of white lateen sails slanting across the blue horizon—a boat race, with dozens of boats. Cast to her forehead, she surveyed them. The boats appeared to move in unison, as if mounted on electric runners, neither gaining ground on those behind nor ceding it to those in front, and for a moment she imagined herself on board one of the boats, feet spread for balance, salt spray breaking over the bow as it sliced through a wave, Steven standing behind her, blocking the wind, and it was such a compelling image that temporarily she forgot what had induced her to create it. When she turned back, Steven was gone, swallowed up by the crowd.

In less than two minutes, she was at the vendor's. She knew she was at the right place; she could smell fried dough and he'd been standing by the vat in which the dough was cooked—she'd marked his position by the round tin chimney rising behind him—and he'd been wearing, what was it? Closing her eyes and tilting her face up to the hot sun, she stood picturing him while the crowd flowed around her. He'd had on an untucked, asparagus-green linen shirt and wrinkled khakis, shoes but no socks, and his hair had been disheveled. So he hadn't expected to see people he knew, or if he had, hadn't cared what they'd think. Suspecting it was the latter, she opened her eyes and rose on her toes and tried to find him.

Searching from side to side, she walked slowly uphill, certain he couldn't have gotten by her to the water. The crowd was too thick for her to move quickly, but after a few minutes it parted suddenly and she saw him across the way, his green-shirted back bent over another table, a camera hanging from his neck.

She was unsure why she'd sought him out. To tell him off? But that would give him the pleasure of thinking it mattered to her, which might be what he wanted. To show that she didn't care, then? But she must have, or she wouldn't have been standing there trying to figure out what to do. Before she could decide, he looked up at her and smiled, and it seemed perfectly natural to walk over and say hello.

In his hand was another pair of binoculars, large and black, and he held them out to her.

"Feel these," he said.

She didn't hesitate; if he was going to pretend nothing had happened, she would, too.

"Heavy as stone, aren't they?"

They were, and she imagined using them for any length of time would be uncomfortable.

"That's why they've never sold well, despite having the most exquisitely calibrated diopters on the market, and some of the best power-to-diameter ratios. See that?" He pointed out white numbers on the black frame, 15X100. "Those indicate the magnification power of the objective lenses, the ones here at the end which point toward what you're looking at, and their diameter, which tells you how big a field they can take in. You want the second number to be at least five times the first, and preferably six or seven."

"And the dioptics?"

"Diopters. The focusing scale on each eyepiece."

He uncapped the lenses and held up the binoculars for her to use, twisting the lenses on their axis so they fit snugly against her eyes, then turned her by the shoulder so she faced the harbor.

"Can you adjust them with only one hand?"

It was the first sign that he'd even noticed her cast. "I think so," she said. "I've had a lot of practice being one-handed recently."

At first her vision was blurred, but gradually, as she twisted the focusing rings and as Steven's hand steadied, she could make out the water. The boats were gone, as if they'd fallen off the edge of the earth, their place taken by endless swells, whose cupped faces caught and reflected sunlight like a series of dunes, and whose ridges turned to glittering spray under a steady wind. She looked for so long the eye caps began to press uncomfortably against the sockets of her eyes, and finally she pulled away.

"Quite remarkable," she said, when she realized how far out she'd been able to see, and in what detail. He was standing very close to her, his chest almost touching her shoulder, and he had on his cologne. She breathed deeply to take in the scent and did not move away. "You know a lot about them."

He recapped the binoculars and recased them, handed them back to the vendor, and steered her away from the table without so much as a word of thanks.

"I collect them," he said, when they were safely out of the vendor's hearing.

"Really? You're the first person I've known who did. It seems an odd thing to collect. How many pairs can you use at once?"

"No odder than pens. How many of those can you use at once?"

So he'd seen her earlier, had been watching what she bought. He had perhaps been too proud to come up to her, fearing rejection, and she understood the feeling; it worked in his favor, indicating an insecurity about her on his part which his speech did not reveal. He took her arm, clasping her elbow with two fingers, just above the cast, which became perceptively heavier at his touch.

"You of course understand why I didn't want that man to hear I was a collector."

"Certainly."

They wound in and out of the crowd, not stopping at tables, talking, while he described for her his interest.

"Binoculars were invented by monks, Capuchins, in the 1600s, for use in war. But the first ones weren't successful, their prisms were two inverting systems, and consequently gave a totally wrong impression of depth, depressions appearing as elevations, and vice versa. They were pseudoscopic, rather than telescopic. For a long time no one could get past that, and for two hundred years they were almost never used."

She learned that, independently, both the Germans and the French eventually solved the problem late in the nineteenth century, just before the start of the Franco-Prussian War, and that binoculars from that time were especially valuable, as were others with military significance. "Death is always a draw," he said. "Collectors like nothing better."

Not always, she thought, surprised to find her mind shifting to its habitual state of opposition. Perhaps residual anger had prompted it, but she did not want to decipher her emotions and steered her thoughts as quickly as possible to an example. Shaker chairs—recently one had gone at auction for nearly two million dollars, and what group had ever had a more vibrant claim to life? But as they walked, she saw the fault in her reasoning. It wasn't Shaker life or the Shakers' love for it that mattered, it was that they were dead, that they could make no more chairs, that increased the value of their remaining goods.

She relaxed and began to enjoy watching Steven talk, his growing animation as he explained the discipline's arcana, exit pupil, relative brightness, field of view, but as he steered her back down the hill, toward the table where she'd first seen him, the smell of fried dough grew stronger; her stomach clenched with hunger, and she realized she'd left her lunch on the shaded stone wall. She thought of trying to retrieve it, but knew it was too late for that now.

Once at the table, he picked up a shiny black leather binocular case, its shoulder strap stiff from lack of use.

"Sixty-five," he said.

The vendor snorted. "One hundred."

"Look, you know yourself the magnification is weak for such a wide lens."

"Eight by forty is standard issue. The Swiss Army uses it, and they don't do anything lightly. It's not as powerful as some, but it's much lighter than most, so you can actually use it longer— which means that, over time, you get a better idea of what you're looking at."

The man took the case back and opened it up, removed the binoculars with no great care, and rested them on his lap, then fished around inside the case. When he pulled out his hand, he was holding four small eyepieces: two purple-shaded lenses, and two yellow ones, which clipped over the eye caps.

"These filters would cost you twenty-five dollars apiece, if you could find them. One's for bright days, like today," he said, holding up the purple pair, "and the other's for night vision. A hundred's a bargain." He put everything back and capped the case and slid it under his table.

"Eighty," Steven said. "They're Russian. Their optics are poorer than Western ones."

"Soviet," the man said. "They never had problems with them in World War Two. The price is fixed. Take it or leave it."

Steven paid, smiling, having known from the start that the price wouldn't be lowered, but acceding willingly to the rules of the exchange.

As they walked away he polished the frames with his shirt. Jean noticed "USSR" written in both the Western and Cyrillic alphabets, a kind of mirror image; it made her think of the Pettigrew account. There was something about it she could use, though at the moment just what it was escaped her.

He put his thumb below the hammer and sickle. "People are throwing these away all over the world because of that symbol. Its connotations make people want to get rid of them." He recased the binoculars and tucked them under his arm. "I hope they do. The fewer there are, the more valuable they become."

"How many do you have?"

"This is my third pair."

"Doesn't that cheapen it for you? Having more than one?" Until today, with the Salz Brothers, she had never contemplated buying multiples of any of her various pens.

"One to sell, one to display, one in case that one breaks."

"And if you sell, do you buy another?"

"No. Once I've sold one, I'm done with it. Three's my limit. It's a perfect number, don't you think?"

They spent an hour winding through the various streets, inspecting the multitude of offerings, neither of them finding anything of interest, until Steven nudged Jean and indicated a heavyset man poking at one of the tables. He was wearing a large floppy hat and khaki shorts and sneakers, and a tape measure protruded from one pocket.

"Decorator," Jean said.

Steven nodded, his attention caught by the man, who'd just given a small shout of glee and was in the process of lifting aside a green metal wastebasket with both hands.

As he put it down, but before his hands were free of it, Steven stepped forward, bumped him aside, and grabbed what the wastebasket had been hiding—a cut-glass candy jar, though at first Jean thought he was reaching for a set of jade bookends. They were lions, about a foot high; the jade was very pale.

"Hey!" the man said. "That's—"

Steven cut him off. "A bottom," he said. "The one on which the other jars rest and therefore rare, since they break easily."

He already had his wallet out, and before the decorator could settle on another line of attack, Steven had read the price on the sticker, extracted the money from his wallet, and paid.

Too late, the decorator saw his opening.

"I'll pay ten dollars more!" he said, reaching for his check-book, but the dealer, a blue-eyed, imperious-looking older woman, who'd had no chance to raise the price since Steven hadn't dickered, was already holding Steven's cash in her up-turned palm; the deal had been completed.

"Thanks," Steven said, nodding at the dealer and ignoring the decorator, then turning away.

Some things Jean did not collect she understood why one might. Black Forest bears, for instance, or sets of Amish hand planes, or rifles from the Spanish-American War, inlaid with sil-ver and ivory. Even the jade bookends. All of them had a certain refined beauty, their weights were pleasing, they fit the hand just so, as objects they felt trued. But there were other things whose collecting mystified her, and candy jars were one of them, mass-produced monstrosities that were awkward to hold, ugly to look at, and frequently clogged with an inextricable mass of hardened jelly beans. Steven's buying it surprised her.

She was about to ask him about it when he said, "I don't like decorators, and I take every opportunity to thwart them. Collecting should be personal and immediate, not corporate and proxied."

It was a feeling she was familiar with: she'd never liked decorators herself, with their tape measures and plastic bags and serially indiscriminate buying sprees, but until now she'd never found anyone else who agreed with her.

"Besides," Steven said, dismissively, "they don't collect, they acquire."

And it was true. Decorators read guides and journals from the various fields, they could distinguish between Louis XIV and Louis XV consoles, they got their hands dirty, perhaps, if what they bought was for themselves—though most often it wasn't—and week after week at fairs and flea markets they sorted through old tins and tool chests for crystal doorknobs or decorative hinges or ivory candlestick holders; they argued about prices, inspected Depression glass for flaws by holding it up to the light and porcelain for hidden cracks by tapping it against wood, but none of that made them collectors. One could finish a room though never a collection, and that seemed to Jean to be a certain dividing line, but more than that, decorators purchased names and looks, not desires; the things they bought they did not have to have.

It was a fundamental difference, Jean thought, and ultimately a profound one. That Steven thought so, too, was another point in his favor. She felt herself moving closer to him.

As they walked, Steven held the jar out so the cut glass caught the light.

"Claudia will like this," he said. "It will be a fine addition to her collection."

"Claudia?" Jean said, stopping. "She collects?"

"You didn't know?"

"Well, she used to. But those?"

"I agree," he said, tucking it under his arm and walking on. "They're not my taste. And I knew they wouldn't be yours. But one should always get the gift one deserves."

They walked a long way to escape the crowds, down the steep winding streets to the harbor, then up others leading out of town, a direction she'd never gone. They were moving away from the boats, which surprised her, but even so the smell of fish was strong; huge chunks of granite lined the shore, with shops and houses built on top of them, painted white, tufts of green grass poking up at their corners; everything else was gray. It was different from the central part of town, the area she was accustomed to, where the houses were painted the colors of the rocks and sea: slate gray, spinach green, a pale, dusty blue. Steven walked quickly, the camera bumping against his chest, his bare ankles showing between his pants and shoes, the left one nearly covered by a scab. Jean had to hurry to keep up with him, and the climbing pulled at her calves.

At one point a line of pelicans flew over, and she ducked at the passage of their shadows, which was so sudden it felt as though someone was about to strike her.

"Pelicans," she said, and counted them. Fifteen.

Steven stopped to follow their flight. Each one seemed to rise up over an invisible bar of air as it crossed from land to sea, and then dropped suddenly, nearer to the surface of the water. "They're unusual here. Blown up the coast by a storm, most likely."

She watched them move off over the water, the rare, indolent flapping of their wings, a motion that passed sequentially from the first bird to the last, and the elegant way that between wing-beats they glided just above the curling waves with their wings veed and still, their bodies canted into the wind, until they were small gray specks in the distance.

At a marine supply store, Steven asked her to wait while he ducked in for something, but she shook her head and laughed. "Oh no you don't. I'm not falling for that again."

The low-ceilinged store smelled of turpentine, and it was so dark she had to stop in the doorway while her eyes adjusted, and by the time they did, Steven had already placed a gallon of white hull paint and some batteries on the nicked and dented counter. There were stacks of coiled rope, dozens of bright slickers, rows of shiny brass instruments, shelves of cleansers and bleaches, but Steven seemed not to notice any of it; he had what he wanted and was ready to go. She was attracted to the rope: the different braids and thicknesses all had different names and, she assumed, different uses, and she could see herself beginning to learn about them, but she made herself turn away.

Outside, she leaned back against the door frame as Steven started off. Racks of blue-and-white-striped cotton sweaters hung on either side of her, which seemed inappropriate, given the day. It was noon, and the sun was directly overhead, hot on her chest and shoulders, so hot that even the sound of waves slapping against the harbor rocks wasn't cooling. She was hungrier than ever.

"Steven," she said, holding her purse against her bare thighs with both hands. Inside were her pens, and it seemed a long time ago that she'd bought them. "Where are we going?"

He stopped and turned back to her, then pointed with the paint can up the road to where it curved around a rocky point. Waves of heat shimmered on the pavement; beyond and behind them was the shining sea. "My house. Don't you know? It's right nearby."

What about my hand? And never calling? And not returning my car? They were questions he should answer, if only she would ask them.

"You are coming, aren't you?" he said. He was still holding out the paint can. Though it must have been getting heavy, his face showed no sign of strain, and his arm wasn't shaking; he seemed enormously strong. She let him wait a few seconds longer and then pushed off the door frame with her shoulders.

"Certainly," she said. She could ask her questions at his house as easily as she could out here in the sun.

"Wait," he said. He set the paint can down and it thunked against the pavement. Beside it he placed the candy jar and the binoculars. Lifting his camera from his chest, he motioned to her with his free hand. "Stand back like that again, will you? Between those racks of sweaters? It's a great shot."

She did as he requested, flattered and somewhat embarrassed.

"Good," he said. "Now tilt your face up, just a bit."

Shade moved down over her hair to her forehead, and then it covered her eyes, and she closed her eyelids and listened to the waves. She could smell the cotton of the sweaters.

"That's it!" he said. "Perfect. Keep still."

Listening carefully, she could just make out the repeated clicking of the camera behind the steady rhythm of the waves, and she saw the scene as if observing it from far above: the woman with one arm in a cast and her face in shadow, as if she'd lost her head, and the man standing in the sun with a paint can and binoculars and a glass candy jar beside his ankle, capturing her on film.

HIS HOUSE, LOW EXCEPT FOR TWO TALL CHIMNEYS ON THE north side, crouched near the brow of a hill as if it had burrowed there. Behind it was a ring of stones, the base of a former lighthouse, Steven explained, one of many that had once dotted the coast and then fallen into disrepair. This lighthouse had been dismantled long ago, its bricks used to face various houses in town; he'd seen a photograph of it, and two or three paintings, but not even the town's oldest residents remembered it. The house itself was white, with a line of blue shutters closed over a bank of windows across the front, and one of its chimneys was smoking.

Over patchy grass and outcroppings of stone they climbed toward the house, which had no neighbors, just scrubby growth where the hill dropped away to the road, and then beyond that rocks and weeds which fell sharply to the water. She admired the view from the front porch while his keys jangled in the door behind her, wood smoke whipping around her in the wind. Curving points of rock jutted out from the north and south, and here, away from the harbor, there was a high, bright sea, its waves not clearly defined. The steady crash of water meeting land rose occasionally to a roar, as a curling wave reflected sound, and then, in breaking, crushed it.

He unlocked the door and invited her in.

With the windows shuttered, the front room was nearly as dark as the inside of the marine supply store, and she waited in the entrance to get her bearings. Beyond the rectangle of light thrown by the open door was the glow of the fire, and the room smelled damp and salty—as if normally it was underwater, but just now the tide was out—and a bit smoky from the fire, which guttered in the wind.

"A hot day for a fire, isn't it?" she asked. Even so she had to resist the elemental pull of the low yellow flames, the urge to go and warm herself beside them.

"I suppose it is," he said, moving about in one of the darkened corners. "But even the hottest days can get cold out here, and I like to be prepared."

She could make out a brass floor lamp, the contours of a couch, some taller furniture looming beyond it, and what appeared to be prints or photographs covering the walls: reflected firelight flickered off glass in a changing pattern, as if a host of fireflies had been trapped indoors and—seeking release—was moving restlessly about.

"Were you expecting someone?"

"You, actually," he said, reentering the light carrying a basket.

"Me?"

"Because of the fair." He set the basket on the back of the couch and moved toward the fire. "I've seen you there before. I thought we clicked rather well, and even though I didn't hear from you after we sailed, I was convinced we'd talk again. I've lit the fire every Sunday since." He squatted to put another log on the grate.

"Didn't hear from me? Shouldn't you have been the one to call?"

"I did." He stood and faced her, the fire rising behind him, outlining his shoulders, the picture frames growing visible now, too, dozens of them hung cheek by jowl, though their contents remained indistinguishable. "But I always got your machine."

He removed two wineglasses from the basket and did not go on, as if she was supposed to understand what he meant, and she believed she did: she knew the machines were a necessity for business, but in private life they seemed an abomination. She had one, of course, but she always suspected people of using them to screen their calls—as she herself did—and rarely left messages on others' machines.

"I have a picnic ready," he said, tilting a glass at the basket.

She'd managed to ignore her hunger while they walked, but now it returned, so powerfully that at first she failed to recognize that the basket was identical to her own. He saw her looking at it.

"The same, isn't it? As the one you brought to the boat?"

Looking more closely, she discovered that it was, and that covering it was the same blue-and-white-checked oilcloth that had covered hers.

"I thought it should be," he said, "since the last time didn't end the way it was supposed to."

He raised one corner of the cloth. "Inside, as well. See?" He lifted out the champagne grapes and the curried chicken and the Stilton and St. André, and the two bags of bread from Parini's. Spackies, they'd be, she could discern their conical shapes through the white paper. "Wine's on board, cooling, but I can get you some now, if you'd like."

"Sure of yourself, aren't you." It was not a question.

"And of you." From a wine bucket on the far side of the couch he produced an uncorked bottle and poured the glasses full, the wine chugging because he poured so fast. "Let me show you something else I think you'll like. Close your eyes," he said.

She laughed nervously and wouldn't do as he asked.

"Trust me," he said, holding out a glass. "I've got a surprise for you."

"I tend not to like surprises."

"I'd guessed that. But unless I miss my mark, you will this one."

She thought of protesting, but decided in the end to submit: she'd come this far, what had she to lose? Dropping the last of her defenses, she closed her eyes. Immediately, his presence drew nearer, his hip bumping against hers as he passed behind her, stirring in her a memory of their sex, at once both baffling and arousing. "Hold your glass steady," he said, putting it in her hand. "And come this way."

His fingers were warm through her blouse, pressing against her waist when he wanted her to turn. "Small steps, so you don't trip."

Her shoes knocked on the wooden floor and she listened for tonal changes to tell her when she was close to furniture or a wall. He gripped her more tightly. "Wait here," he said. "And keep your eyes closed." He did not let go until she agreed.

She felt him move away, a palpable tug. He stepped outside,

and then came the clacking of wood on wood; she guessed it was the shutters folding open as light flooded over her. His footsteps reapproached and she sipped from her wine.

"Bend down," he said, holding one hand before her eyes. She smelled smoke on his skin, and the wine, and dust. "About forty-five degrees. But slowly. You don't want to bump into anything." His other hand was at her back.

She did as he asked.

"Good. Now open your eyes and look."

The light was blinding, and at first she had a hard time distinguishing anything. Then she saw a pair of olive-green binoculars inches from her face, mounted in reverse on a metal stand, so that she would be looking in through the wrong end.

"There goes the diamond," she said, and laughed.

Behind the binoculars' magenta-colored lenses, clipped close to the eyepieces, was a picture, which he screened with his hand until she was peering through the lenses.

"Recognize anything?"

It seemed to be a wall, painted taupe or the palest gray.

"No. I'm sorry. I don't. Should I? It looks like dappled paint."

When she started to straighten, he said, "Look again."

She tried, but the picture still didn't resemble anything. It might have been of a texture rather than of a shape.

He put his thumb and forefinger to the back of her neck and pressed her head closer to the lenses. "Describe it, then."

Annoyed, resisting the pressure of his fingers, she said, "An expanse of color, off-white, tan maybe, dimpled like the surface of a golf ball. It has a streak of pure white, traveling diagonally from bottom left to top right."

"Excellent." When he released her, her head snapped back a few inches.

"Well, that was fascinating," she said. Straightening, she could feel the residual touch of his fingertips on her neck as distinctly as if they'd made individual impressions in warm wax. He hadn't stepped back. The fire popped, and looking at it, she was aware of him watching her.

"It should be," he said, picking up his glass. "It's you."

"What?" She checked herself from bending for another look.

"Sorry," he said, and smiled, aware, it seemed, that he'd been too forceful. He moved aside. "It's a picture of you."

He lifted the picture from behind the binoculars and handed it to her. Circled by a black rim, the area outside it blurred, she sat on a white chair holding a coffee mug with both hands. Her head was tilted back, her face turned up to the sun, and over her shoulders was a sweater. Her long neck looked exposed.

"Examining pictures through binoculars, you learn much

more about people than you think you could. Right here, for instance." His finger went to her throat, just above her larynx, and arced across her skin. "You have a crescent-shaped scar. It barely shows in this light, but it's very pretty, and that's the streak of white you saw in the picture."

Her pulse pushed against his nail, and the attention was oddly flattering. No one had ever paid such close regard to her skin, not even she herself, and she ran her hand over the binoculars on the stand to hide her embarrassment.

"I imagine that scar is something you got in one of your games with Claudia."

It was possible, she did not remember acquiring it, though most of the others in her collection she did. The semicircular one above her left elbow, the fat one wobbling across her right forearm, the long shiny one that ran down her back like a second spine, she remembered which of each of their various games had produced those scars, where she'd stumbled or fallen, when she'd been pushed.

The line of four still healing across the back of her fingers, black and raised, was, of course, courtesy of Steven.

He took the picture from her and replaced it in the stand. A series of binoculars and pictures was spread out across a long trestle table, which stretched the width of the room, in front of the bank of windows. Eight pairs of binoculars mounted in reverse on steel stands and one empty stand, the stands clustered in groups of three. All of the binoculars had pictures fixed behind them, and each had a different case: brushed steel, black plastic, olive-green rubber. As she watched, he mounted the pair of Soviet binoculars he'd bought earlier on the last stand, and now it was the only one without a picture. She was standing at the one before it.

"Where did you get it?"

"The picture? From the fair. A while back."

"Before we went sailing?"

"Oh no. After."

He adjusted a pair of camouflaged binoculars on its stand and did not meet her gaze; it was the first time she had not believed him. Her disbelief gave her a sense of power: he was willing to lie to her, he had something to hide. Hadn't he said upon first meeting her that he'd been watching her for a while? She'd taken it then to mean during the reception, but now she wasn't so sure; perhaps he'd been at it longer.

"I wanted to use one shot on the boat, but none of those came out, and Claudia said she'd send me some from the wedding, but I haven't heard from her."

"I see."

She moved to her left and did not think about it. The next picture, the one beside her own, was of an indeterminate seascape: white-capped water, gray cliffs, green hills. Like all the other pictures, it, too, had a clear central portion ringed in black, as if it had been meant for a circular frame.

"Where's this?" she said, and bent to look at it. Through the lens appeared a wall of gray.

"That's a spot I've found. I hope you'll like it."

"I'm sure I will." Her words felt somewhat forced, and he seemed aware of it.

"I haven't offended you, have I?" He waited until she looked up at him. He was solicitous, yet growing distant again; he seemed to be watching her from some remove. It hadn't taken him long to recover. "It's just that I find you beautiful."

She smiled her thanks.

"Listen." He put his glass down and rubbed his hands together in an attempt to be hearty. "Let me make it up to you. Another sail. We'll go this afternoon."

She'd fantasized about this moment, believing it would offer her a chance to return the favor of humiliation, but now that it was here, she realized she'd hoped for the invitation not because she wanted to hurt him, but because she wanted to go.

She turned her wrist over and looked at her watch to give herself time, not wanting to reveal her interest too quickly. A few minutes to one. "We won't have time, will we?"

"It doesn't take long to ready the boat."

"Only to clean it up."

He didn't take the bait.

"Perhaps tomorrow would be better," she said.

"No. Definitely not tomorrow." The forcefulness of his voice startled her. "Tomorrow is going to be too rough. A storm's coming, they'll have a small-craft advisory up, and nothing under a hundred feet should be out."

"But the weather's beautiful."

"Look up there." He pointed to a few white fingers of clouds far above the ocean, too high up and too thin yet to cast shadows, blurred through the salt-sprayed glass. "Those are the harbingers, the first sign of low pressure. The surf's already rising.

"And hear that?" In the background, by concentrating, coming from the interior of the house, she could make out a droning voice and patches of static—a radio. It surprised her that she hadn't noticed it before.

"It's tuned to the weather station. They're talking about tomorrow, what kind of day it will be."

Even straining to hear it, she could distinguish only stray

words. *Knots; seas; sustained winds.* Repeated toward the end of the message was *Pig and Sow islands.*

"It's going to be a storm."

"Won't the water be rough today, then?"

"It could be. But nothing dangerous, certainly. Much as it was the first day we went out. Besides, tomorrow's Monday. You'd have to work." He picked up their glasses from the table and wiped away the condensation rings with his palm. "But I understand that you might not be interested. It's simply better if you say so."

"No, it's not that." She squared her shoulders and looked again at the picture of the sea, and at the picture of herself. "It's not that at all."

"Let's go, then."

Without answering, she walked down the line of pictures, examining them, and heard a distant church clock strike one; services would be over, people spilling from the church doors, dressed in their Sunday finery, chattering as they emerged into the sunlight. She preferred being here.

The first group of pictures seemed to feature a woman, a redhead who was otherwise nondescript, and the first and third pictures, despite slight differences, appeared to be of the same stretch of sea. Water, the woman, and water again, swells and whitecaps, with a smudge of color in the center of the third. She inspected it more closely. A buoy, a pale orange speck bobbing on the crest of a wave.

"Who's this?" she said, indicating the woman's picture with her cast. Her round face was circled in black.

"My wife."

"Oh God," she said. "You're not married, are you?" The possibility appalled her, it had never crossed her mind.

"Widowed."

"Good." She put her hand to her chest, then recovered, remembering her manners. "Forgive me." She fiddled with the cast. "It's just that—"

He stopped her, hand raised. "Don't explain, I understand. Married men aren't anyone's idea of a wise date."

"May I ask what happened?"

"An accident," he said, turning away with the glasses toward the entrance to the rest of the house, which she took to mean he wished not to discuss it.

The other group of pictures clustered on the table seemed arty. All three were of a wooden floor, though the second also had a single woman's shoe in one corner, lying on its side. The picture was shot from above but lit from below, so that the white shoe and its broken heel cast long shadows on the caramel-colored wood. In the third picture, the wood was redder, as if shot in afternoon light, or through a filter.

Around the rest of the room were dozens of binoculars, mounted on frames, hanging from rafters, standing on their cases, so many that he could have opened a shop. The pictures on the walls were visible now too, all of women, most taken from a distance. She regarded several.

When he returned, he carried the picnic basket to the door.

"Conquests?" Jean asked, indicating the photos.

"Subjects."

"How come none of the ones on the walls are portraits?"

"Very good," he said, approaching her. "I knew you had a sharp eye. Only one other woman has noticed that the first time."

"Your wife?"

"My fiancée."

"A wife, and now a fiancée? Interesting. Any others I should know about?"

"No. Just those two. And it's a former fiancée, not a current one."

She lifted a picture from the wall, of a woman sitting in a parked car, studying herself in a compact mirror.

"You've had rather bad luck with your heart," she said.

"Oh no, I've chosen very wisely."

She rehung the picture and rubbed dust from her fingertips. "And how come the ones on the walls aren't looking at the camera?"

He straightened the frame, aligning it with those above and below, and said, "I don't like talking to subjects. It prevents getting the picture I want. Unstudied. They can forget you're there, if you're shooting from a distance."

"Or not even know," Jean said.

"Exactly. And at first that's best of all. Of course, after you get to know them, you can usually get any pose you want, but the unsuspecting ones reveal the most."

Below one picture lay a fountain pen. A Sheaffer, she guessed, by the styling; she recognized the filigree, the brightness of the gold.

She picked it up and unscrewed the heavy cap. Black nib and ends, Sheaffer Number 8 scripted on the pocket clip. Her fingers shook as she turned it. The pen was worth a small fortune, six thousand dollars perhaps.

"Yours?" she said. She had to clear her throat and repeat her question before he heard her.

"That? Oh yes. From the fair. Is it a good one?"

She told him what she thought it was worth. He took it from her and tossed it on the back of the couch.

"Good. I'll have to find a suitable place for it, then."

She went back to the pictures, pretending to be unflustered. She wondered which vendor he'd bought it from, what he'd paid.

Nearby was the candy jar he'd bought for Claudia. It rocked as she rubbed her finger around its rim; the base was slightly uneven, and if she moved her finger quickly enough, it might eventually topple over. She was surprised to find herself considering this, a flare-up of an old jealousy that she'd thought she'd extinguished years ago, with the fire. Her aunt had been right after all; it had been Jean's idea to start that fire, and though Claudia had instantly agreed, it came to Jean now that she had always been the leader, the one to make suggestions, the first to jump or fall.

She released the jar and traced instead the black circle on one of the pictures.

"Why the black circles?" she asked.

"I shot them all through binoculars. It adds another dimension, a certain distance. And it filters out unnecessary details. That one, for instance," he said, gesturing at the woman with the compact resting on her raised palm. "I wanted that woman's face as she scrutinized herself. If she was in the city or at the beach, if it was raining or sunny or cold, none of that mattered. She was fascinated by her own reflection—mirrors do that to people—and I had to capture that without her knowing, and without extraneous material to distract the viewer."

Jean looked again at the binoculars clustered on the table, the Soviet one alone bereft of a picture. She should probably call Bonnie about her idea for the Pettigrew account; it was a good one.

"Listen," he said. "Could you do me a favor?" Once again he was holding out the picture of her. "Sign this?"

"Certainly. May I use the Sheaffer?" Since she'd begun collecting she'd hoped to find one, and she suspected this was the closest she would ever come.

"Sorry," he said, producing a recent Waterman, slim and cobalt blue. At any other time, she'd have found it beautiful. "No ink for the Sheaffer. It's a bladder pen, and I only have cartridges. And for signing pictures, this actually works better."

She hesitated, unsure whether to believe him, then took the offered pen and bent over the picture, meaning to sign it on the throat, just above the scar. "Your choice," she said. To have a pen like that and not use it seemed almost obscene.

With his thumb and forefinger, he squeezed her wrist to stop her.

"The back, please. I don't want anything to mar the face."

She turned it over and wrote her name. The ink blobbed, but it could have been from her nerves. He blew on the signature to dry it, then returned the picture to its stand.

Lifting the basket from the floor, he said, "Ready?"

She walked a little way away from him, allowing herself time to consider. She rested the cast on the back of the couch near the pen, surveyed the room with its pictures and binoculars, breathed deeply, and said, "All right, let's go."

He ducked his head, appearing excited but not grateful, which relieved her. Had he done so, she might have changed her mind. As it was, she flexed her fingers, her hand left the couch, and she was ready.

THE DOCKS WERE UNCROWDED, THE OFFICE DESERTED; they would be underway in half an hour. Jean elected to wait in the office with the basket while Steven prepped the boat. The wind was steadily rising; even from inside the office she could hear its peculiar metallic whistling, like an antenna whipping through the air, and the bay was choppy, each wave crest bright with sun. The air smelled saltier than usual.

She stood by a folding chair and took out her own pens and turned them in her palm, and, finding them suddenly pedestrian beside the Sheaffer, regretted having bought them. One brilliant pen was better than an entire collection of above-average ones. The basket she pushed away with her foot, determined not to look inside. It scraped over the loose linoleum, and when it was out of immediate reach she felt better, as she did not want to eat until the appointed time, and found it too much of a temptation nearby.

The office was shabby, smelling of smoke and burnt coffee,

with unwashed windows and layers of papers curled on corkboards like chipping paint. She had expected more glamour. On the plastic table beside her lay a stack of brochures from a charter service. *"One fish, Two fish, We fish, You fish."* She decided to check her answering machine.

She had six new messages, and she pressed the code to hear them.

The first was a hang-up, the second someone who listened for thirty seconds without speaking. "She?" a woman's voice said in the third one. "It's Me." Claudia's voice surprised her into sitting.

"The honeymoon was great," she said. "We got home late last night. Miles of beaches and no people, except for beggars, who were everywhere once we got off the boat, selling everything. Or trying to. At first it was vexatious as hell, since they spoke an indecipherable English, but if you ignored them long enough they'd leave you alone. Then they'd sit there beside you, talking back and forth, and after a while it got relaxing, not knowing what they were saying, letting the rhythm of the sounds wash over you like the sea. You have to go, maybe next year with both of us, or just you and me if Boyd can't do it. You could bring a date. I'm so black I look like I was turned on a spit."

She went on about her honeymoon and Jean only half listened, finding herself mentally rearranging the contents of the basket, removing the Spackies, handling the wine, never touching the pen, which she'd dropped in after Steven had left the basket with her. She wondered what he'd think when he found it—he must have known she'd be unable to resist it. After a long passage about sharks near a reef they dove on, Claudia said, "Tomorrow, I want you to come over and look at pictures from the trip. I'll have the wedding pictures, too. I just got them back. And that reminds me, are you still seeing Steve—*Mr. Accident?* How's that going?" She went on a little longer, and then asked Jean to call her.

The next message was from someone who'd confused her number with the funeral parlor's, a man who introduced himself and then asked if someone could pick up his mother at Sacred Heart Nursing Home, as if she'd been out for a day of shopping and needed a ride back.

She didn't want to hear the rest of it, or any of the other messages, and she forwarded through it and erased them all and briefly closed her eyes. She was tired. She could go home and catch up on her sleep, she didn't have to get on that boat, though of course leaving would entail explanations and she had none handy. Leaning back against the wall, she found the plaster bumpy beneath her skull. Now wasn't the time to sleep. Long ago, at the last joint birthday party with Claudia, Uncle Teddy had told them not to waste their lives by sleeping. There'd be time enough for that when they were dead.

She sat up and took out the binoculars Steven had left with her, the stiff leather case creaking as she opened it, fitted the binoculars to her eyes and looked at Steven, then at other boats, most of which were battened down. The *Lucky Lady* was one of them, which didn't surprise her. Well, perhaps this was her day to get lucky. She raised the binoculars to the horizon. A few clouds showed where the water met the sky, but the waves seemed manageable, nothing she couldn't survive.

She focused on Steven again. As he mopped the deck, he pushed a yellow plastic bucket over the wood with his instep. He scrubbed the deck thoroughly from bow to stern, then went over it again from side to side. He'd put his shoes on the dock so they wouldn't mark the deck, and she could see the scab on his ankle clearly; it tapered toward the top, like a pine tree. When he was done, he held onto a cleat and leaned over the gunwale to pour the water out.

She wished she had the camera, since Steven deserved to have his picture taken, too, but it was the one thing he'd held on to; she wanted to capture his rapt, oblivious expression as he worked. It was him, that expression. She found it odd that Claudia had called him Steve. The name didn't fit, since nothing for him was a shortcut, and he was not the type of person whose name one abbreviated or to appreciate having it done. Claudia must not have known him well.

That was disappointing. Jean had hoped for more from her cousin, but then it had been years since they'd really talked, and perhaps Claudia had changed in unfortunate ways. One could not expect of others what one did of oneself.

She flipped the binoculars and looked again at the spare white lettering on the black frame, the fun-house mirror image of two languages saying the same thing. That was what the Pettigrew account needed: a new visual gag to spice up the written one. They could run three different ads. A Russian, a Japanese, and maybe an Arab, all looking in the mirror, all fat and bald like their current model, all thinking the same thing, and their thoughts would be written out in their individual languages. The mirrors, of course, would translate their thoughts: *One cannot expect of others what one expects of oneself.* The reader would be in on the joke of the characters' blindness, and the tag could move on without sacrificing its past.

She dialed Bonnie's number, and Bonnie answered on the second ring.

"Bonnie? It's Jean. I've got something to tell you."

"Do I need a pen for it?"

Yes, Jean said, she probably did. Bonnie put down the phone and Jean heard her retreating steps, drawers squeaking open, the rustling of paper. Was this then to be her legacy, reworking an old tag on someone else's behalf, for a product she no longer cared for? Inducing strangers to clutter their lives with one more "thing"? It was not the way she could foresee her life ending. The amount of work it would take tired her. Putting the binoculars aside, she opened the basket and found the pen. She decided that there was little difference between that kind of life and Mrs. Olsen's, standing in the box of her hallway behind the closed door, listening to other lives go on outside it, and neither life held much appeal.

"Bonnie?" she said. She had to repeat it a few times before Bonnie came back to the phone. "Never mind. I've got one here." She twirled the Sheaffer in her fingers. "I'll just write you a note about it. I won't be in on Monday."

"Jean," Bonnie said. Then she was quiet. The buzzing that filled the silence seemed to Jean to be the sound of Bonnie thinking, but evidently Bonnie was letting her disapproval sink in. "You've missed a lot of work recently. That's not a good sign."

"Don't worry about signs, Bonnie. Worry about my work."

"They've been five good years," Bonnie said, ignoring her. "Healthy years. You don't want to lose that, do you?"

Jean listened to herself breathe into the phone. When it became obvious she would not respond, Bonnie cleared her throat.

"Listen. I'm not going to fight with you about this. I'm too old to play soldier."

She sneezed, and then said, "Oh yes. Your mother called."

"My mother? How do you know her?"

"I don't. But she hadn't heard from you for a long time. She was worried."

"The only thing she's worried about is her husband."

"Your father?"

"Her husband. My father's dead. He died years ago."

There was silence.

"Christ," Jean said finally.

"I told her about your accident," Bonnie said.

"Oh, that's perfect. That should set her off nicely."

"It's your own mother," Bonnie said. "You're a pretty cold fish."

"I was raised in a pretty cold sea."

"Speaking of which, are you going sailing today?" Bonnie asked.

Jean didn't have a ready answer, and her pause was all Bonnie needed. "Enjoy," she said, and hung up.

Jean gripped the receiver until the dial tone returned, then packed the binoculars and put away the pen and looked around the room. It had nothing to hold her. She picked up the basket and went out the door and down the open steps toward the boat.

Steven snapped a line tight around a cleat. When he saw Jean he hopped from the deck to the dock and took her arm.

"You can leave the basket and binoculars here; it's safe. The last of the supplies will be coming from the store in a minute."

They walked halfway down the dock to meet the delivery boy, who was tall and seemed to have recently grown out of his pants; several inches of shin showed above his sneakers. Steven tipped him, then took items from the bag and laid them one at a time on the dock and checked them against his list. Air freshener, bleach, a bag of cotton rags.

Jean looked up at the sound of someone approaching and recognized the short man she'd seen weeks before on the dock, when she'd come to retrieve her car. He was still pink-skinned, though an unhealthy white showed where he'd recently shaved his beard. Apple Jacks and Frosted Flakes and a box of powdered donuts stuck up from the bag of groceries he was holding.

"You're going out with him?" he asked, nodding at Steven. He looked appalled.

"Yes," she said. "While the weather's still good."

"Weather won't affect your trip."

She plucked the Apple Jacks out of his bag. "And I see good health won't interfere with your diet."

The delivery boy blushed and studied the money in his palm, as if expecting it to change into something else, and the short man drew himself up to his full height, which didn't quite reach Jean's chin. "My diet isn't your concern."

"And our trip isn't yours."

He opened his mouth to respond, then grabbed the Apple Jacks from her and stuffed them back in his bag. She scooped up their purchases and moved away.

By the boat, she balanced on one foot and removed a shoe. "Do you know that man?"

"I see him here from time to time," Steven said. "But beyond that, no."

"Does he work here?" She slipped off the other shoe and handed the pair to Steven. They had been fine for the flea market and during the long hike to Steven's house, and then here, to

the docks, but heels could get tricky on the boat, where she preferred the surer grip of bare skin.

"I hope not. He hardly seems competent." He lifted the basket to the deck. "Shall we go?"

She shook her head. She had chosen this path, but he would
not hurry her down it. She still wanted a few questions answered.

"He said the owner of your boat had gone to heaven."

Steven consulted a pocket chart of times and tides and his
watch, which had only four hours marked on it, nine, ten,
eleven, and twelve, as if time for him was compressed into only
brief spans that mattered, and at last said, "That's true. I tried
selling it for a while after my wife died, but had no luck."

He took the grocery bag from her and tossed it aboard. It
skittered to a stop and tipped over, but nothing spilled onto the
deck. "Ready?" He held out his hand.

The wind was blowing. She had to pull her hair out of her
eyes and tuck it behind her ears to see him, and the club flags
snapped in the stiffening breeze. Was she ready for this? It was
odd how flags of the same size rippled differently. She could turn
away now, the wind could be her excuse, the water after all was
going to be rougher. Standing on the dock, smelling the salt air,

she found that this last step onto the swaying boat suddenly felt enormous.

As she hesitated, the dock began to tremble with someone's approach, the wood shifting beneath her feet as if she stood on one end of a seesaw while a child jumped on the other. It was the short man again, and she didn't want to talk to him. She took Steven's hand and climbed on board.

"Can I give you some advice?" the man said, pausing beside the boat, groceries clutched to his chest. He was watching her as she bobbed above him on the deck, staring at her eyes. Looking back at him, she wondered if he'd ever had a booth at a flea market.

"Tell him to go away, will you?" Jean asked. Her feet were damp, and she didn't dare move just yet, afraid she'd slip on the polished wood. "I don't want to hear what he has to say," she said.

"Don't be foolish." The short man shook his head. "You really ought to know these things." He gestured with the groceries at the boat. "Just listen to me for a minute." The bag rustled as he clasped it again to his chest.

Steven stepped in front of him. He was a full foot taller than the man, his shoulders nearly that much wider. "She asked nicely for you to move on."

"No, she didn't. She didn't ask that at all. And what do you know about being polite?"

Jean barely saw Steven's hand, it moved so quickly. Blood erupted from the man's nose, so much of it that it looked fake, and she realized she'd heard a sound like shells being crushed underfoot when the heel of Steven's palm connected with the man's face. Then the man was kneeling on the gray planks, his groceries spilled around him, and a widening V down the front of his white shirt was changing to red in a matter of seconds, the color so shiny it looked cellophaned.

Watching the incident from the bobbing deck of the boat she felt hollow and miles away. It was sunny and the water was bright and all of this was happening on a television set with poor reception, to other people in another time. It seemed no more connected to her life than any of the events she saw daily on the news or read about in the paper.

"Will you go now?" Steven asked, standing over the man. His voice was level, neutral. He might have been asking the time.

The man nodded and disks of bright blood dripped onto the weathered boards in front of him, and Steven put his palm to the man's forehead and gently pushed it back until the man's face tilted skyward. He had a goatee of blood, even his teeth were coated. Steven plucked the man's handkerchief from his pocket and pressed it to his nose and lips.

"Hold your head back like this when you walk, and when you get somewhere you can lie down, pinch the nostrils as hard as you can without pushing back on the bone. It sounded like it broke."

He put his hands under the man's armpits and hoisted him to his feet, gathered his bag of groceries and handed it to him, and turned him on his way. The man stumbled twice, unable to see where he was walking, but didn't fall.

Steven set the binoculars on board, loosened the mooring lines, and jumped onto the deck. Blood speckled the front of his shirt. Jean's hand ached, and looking down she realized she'd balled her fists; she spread her fingers and shook her hand.

"Shall we go, then?" Steven asked, as if nothing had happened. The bumpers squeaked as a swell pushed the boat against them, and the deck tilted; Steven reached to steady her, his fingers digging into her biceps. Across one of his knuckles the skin was split, the blood already darkening as it dried.

He positioned her to the side, a dance she recalled from the last outing, when he'd moved her around as he needed to tighten lines or trim the sails, and a gull cried above them, causing her to look up into the sky. Clouds were moving toward them, fat and pewter gray, but most of the sky was blue. As she tracked the gull's flight across it, the crescent scar on her throat seemed to thicken and glow, and she knew the picture Steven had asked her to sign was from before she'd even met him, or, at the latest, from the Sunday she'd spent at the fair, angry that he hadn't called; in it, her hand had been free of a cast. When he'd approached her on the lawn that first day, that meant, holding his glass of champagne, he'd already singled her out.

That was as it should be, she thought; like the best collectors—as her father had once told her—he was thorough in everything he did.

The engine coughed, sputtered, caught, and the smell of exhaust briefly replaced that of salt air. She sat as they backed out of the slip, so that at first Steven was looking over her while he steered, beyond her at the colorful sterns and tangled masts of the boats moored along the other docks, and then he reversed the engine, spun the wheel and increased the throttle, and the exhaust pipe burbled as it cleared the water when the boat leaned into the turn. Salt spray kicked up, dampening her hair and sprinkling her face, and the engine note grew louder; she felt its vibrations through her bare feet.

The sensation made her crane her neck and look back at

Steven's anchorage. Her shoes were there, neatly paired on the edge of the dock, as though someone had stepped out of them and jumped into the water and disappeared. Steven had left them. On one of the pilings they passed was a pair of yellow rubber gloves. Some fisherman had probably lost them and another had found them and placed them on the piling, palms up, for him to find.

She licked the salt from her lips and in no time they had moved beyond the long sweeping curve of the stone jetty, and then they were headed for the sea. They seemed to be passing by the rocks in the harbor faster than she remembered, the fluorescent lobster floats and the lighted navigation buoys, but she told herself that memory has its own language, and, like others, it could become corrupted.

She tucked her bare feet under her; despite the sunlight, the wooden deck was chilly, and goosebumps had appeared on her thighs. Perhaps it was just anticipation that made her perceive this trip as happening more quickly than the last one, though she doubted that was the case. Steven would want to hurry now, too; the weather was closing in.

She watched him record the time on a chart as they cleared the harbor, and then she shut her eyes in order to make the first part of the journey in the dark.

WITH THE ENGINE CUT, THE BOAT ROCKED ON THE SWELLS, and Jean's stomach rocked with it, seeking its balance. She put her drink down, the wine sliding up the glass and lipping over the rim onto her fingers.

"Really, I'd like to talk about it," she said, rubbing her biceps with her cupped palm as she spoke, her hand moving in bursts.

"No," Steven said. He dropped the anchor and they both watched the rope play out while the anchor sank, twirling into the green water. A scattering of low, puffy clouds blocked the sun occasionally, turning the cool wind cold, and she could almost taste the salt air.

"Why not?" She was still looking at the rope disappearing into the water. She had always known that in making certain choices one committed oneself to a sequence of actions—which inevitably meant a switch from being master of one's fate to being its slave—but she had hoped that she could decide when to make that switch, instead of having it forced upon her. Talking would put things off a little longer. It was like collecting, that way: the thrill was in the chase, not the finish. For her, she realized. For him it would be different.

"It's nothing," he said, knotting the tightened rope around a cleat with his bandaged hand. "And I don't like to talk about it." She had brought it up on the ride out and he was tired of discussing it.

Directly north stood the shore, a series of steep, striated granite cliffs leading to low green hills. Shading his eyes, he looked toward land. A flock of gulls was diving, about halfway in, several birds breaking off from the flock to investigate the boat, and he thought he could see a few small black figures moving about on the hills, mysteriously purposeful, like ants, but they were too far off to make out, even through the binoculars. And there might have been a church steeple, though perhaps it was a smokestack, or simply a small, drifting cloud, but he hadn't the patience to wait and see, or to check the charts for landmarks.

"Well," he said, clapping. "We should eat." He squeezed her shoulder from behind, spotting her blouse with blood, and slipped past her to get the food.

She knelt, trying to concentrate on separating the extra-thick paper plates he insisted on, but her hands felt clumsy and she couldn't pry the plates apart.

"What's the matter?" He appeared from belowdecks with a platter of cheese and grapes.

She was staring at the plates. "Nothing," she said. When she looked up, the Sheaffer was in the middle of the platter. "It's just a little—"

"Seasickness?"

"Yes." She turned the plates over and laid them on the deck. With her fingers spread, she could nearly reach from edge to edge. She leaned her weight on them until they buckled. "That's it. Seasickness."

"Let's sit down then."

He steered her to the stern by her shoulders, around the cabin, over a bound sail, and had her sit against the gunwale, knees apart, head down. He claimed that always worked. She was still holding her wine.

Eyes closed, she heard him moving about, securing the sails, sweeping the galley, tapping the compass's glass housing with his fingernails. His shoes squeaked over the teak decking. Minutes passed. The hypnotic rhythm of the swells slapping the side of the boat began to calm her, and she realized after a while that every fourth wave was louder. She felt their tiny blows in her back first, then the boat rising beneath her thighs and feet, and her stomach counterbalancing.

He lifted her hair from her eyes and said, "Feeling better?"

She wasn't but said she was, knowing it would please him.

He crouched and smiled at her, rubbing her knees with his palms, which made her shiver. She'd liked the way he did that when they first met.

"Tell me again, please," she said. "How did your first wife die?"

His face darkened, but this time he sighed, and she knew he would answer.

"My only wife."

"Yes. Forgive me. Your only wife."

"I forgive you."

"Please do."

"I said I did."

"Yes, you did, didn't you? You said you did. Your only wife."

"So far." He smiled and ruffled her hair. His bandage snagged on her knotted scarf and her entire scalp tingled; she thought he'd grasp her head with his other hand to free it, but when he snapped his wrist, the bandage jerked loose from her scarf.

She resisted the urge to smooth her hair. "How was it again?"

"On a boat."

"This boat?"

"Yes."

"I thought it wasn't on the boat."

"We were sailing. She fell overboard." He nodded at the water, as if this were the very spot. "Bad luck."

"Did they find her?"

"Never."

"They wouldn't, would they?"

"What's that supposed to mean?" He stood, knees clicking as he rose, and she could hear him breathing. His shoes shone as if they'd just been polished, and his cologne was stronger than she remembered.

"The ocean's so big, and a body so small. It's a wonder they find anyone out here."

He stepped away and adjusted the wheel, as the boat had drifted athwart the waves.

"How sad," she said.

"Yes. It's very hard."

"I was thinking of her family, not having a grave to go to."

"Family's overrated."

In the silence, a wave smacked against the weather side of the boat, especially loud, as if someone was about to board and had struck the planking with an open palm as a signal. Steven seemed not to notice. The deck tilted beneath Jean from the wave's impact, and she raised her eyes as if expecting someone's head to pop up beside her, but no one was around, of course, just the heavy swells, rolling toward them on one side and away on the other, into the blinding sun.

He was readying his camera. By his foot was the locker where he stored the life jackets, though she knew she wouldn't need one. She looked out at the water and the distant shore. She had seen it in Steven's picture, but it was still unfamiliar, territory she knew now she would never explore.

"Could you tell me where we are?"

"Offshore."

"Where, exactly? I'd just like to know the spot."

"I can't say, really. Far enough out, deep enough water. It's safe here. Somewhere near Sow Island."

"And your fiancée?" she asked.

He rested the camera against his hip and squinted into the sun. "A ladder. She was changing a light bulb on the second-floor hall landing."

"And you let go."

"The phone rang. It was," he said, and paused, his free hand working as he searched for the right word, "instinctual."

"The shoe in the picture?" she said.

"Hers. Her neck broke, if you're interested. I knew she was

dead because her eyes were open but not moving. The eyes of the dead don't reflect light."

He put the camera down and peeled the bandage from his hand. A knuckle showed through the split skin, white and glistening, like a tooth. When he flexed his fingers, drops of blood arced toward her bare foot and one landed in her wine, where it diffused slowly. He swore.

His footsteps retreated, thumping down the stairs to the cabin, and then came close again. The rag he used to clean the blood smelled of bleach and its odor stung her nostrils. It occurred to her that he was preparing the boat for a sale, not to sail it.

She wondered if Claudia might come to feel guilty about having introduced them, and remembered how her green dress had clung to her skin in the heat, and the smell of crushed grass, and the sensation of champagne bubbles popping on her tongue. And Steven, standing in front of the sun so she couldn't see his face.

The afternoon was getting on. Mrs. Olsen would be posting her useless warnings, then shuffling back to her room and waiting for Jean to come home. She'd listen for the familiar footsteps passing by her door, note whether Jean's mail had been taken in, and by five tomorrow afternoon, at the latest, she would call the police. It had happened several times before, once when she was still seeing Oliver Brisbane.

Steven began to talk to her. The decking shone in the sun and it was too dazzling to look at for long, but she would not close her eyes, not now. She wanted to see what was coming. Still, the light was trance-inducing; though she knew she should be listening to Steven, in the back of her mind she heard her old chant starting up: *it's a lie, it's a lie, it's a lie.*

Sensing her inattention, he slammed her head against the gunwale. The pain passed quickly, though her back felt strained—the movement had stretched her muscles awkwardly—and her mind was suddenly clear. She screamed, understanding how final her decision was, and then began to cry, which surprised her.

Steven was beside her. But rather than enlarging his anger, which she'd feared, her tears seemed to calm him, as if in crying she had fulfilled an obligation, a necessary step in a long-established protocol, and he could now proceed. He waited patiently beside her for her crying to stop, and then bound his hand with the bleach-soaked rag. She wasn't sure whether the sharp intake of breath she heard was his or her own.

He knelt beside her and produced and uncapped the Sheaffer, and gave it a quick inspection, squinting at the nib, then pulled her arm toward him, the left one, the one without the cast. He shook the pen, distributing the ink, then wrote her name on the soft fleshy underside of the forearm, having to press firmly to get the ink to flow across her skin. The nib, despite its sharpness, caused her no pain, and she noticed again his beautiful hand. When he was done, he blew on the ink to dry it, recapped the pen, and threw it overboard, and though she listened for it, she could not pick up the splash. She thought briefly of her collection, the silver chest propped open, and rank after rank of gleaming pens in the afternoon sunlight.

"Pay attention," he said, resting his hand on her shoulder. It felt light, as it always had, hollow, pieced together from straw and air; his touch was almost friendly.

She tried. She sat up straighter. She wiped her face and wondered what Claudia would make of all this, safe as she was, back at her apartment, her candy jars ranged along one wall, and how she would remember it in years to come. If she would have pictures, or only her imagination to rely on. He began to talk again. She rested her weight on the hand with the cast and at first what he said made sense; he was talking about the tides and how you could see them switch if you watched carefully, blue water shifting into green, the flow beginning to run in another direction, and what that meant for objects floating on the surface, but soon his words sounded odd, they might have been from a different language. She had to study his lips and connect their movements with the sounds to understand what he was saying, and after a while the effort became too much—words turned particulate and peculiar, something elemental. The clouds thickened and the wind picked up, rising from an occasional flutter to a steady rattling presence, and she watched the cloud shadows race over the water away from the boat, and soon his words began to disappear in the wind. There was the wind over his words and under them and through them, and suddenly, when he moved his mouth, she couldn't hear any sound from him at all, only the wind.

ABOUT THE AUTHOR

PAUL GRINER's first book was the critically acclaimed story collection *Follow Me*. Griner has master's degrees in Romance languages and literature from Harvard and in creative writing from Syracuse University. He received a Fulbright grant to Portugal and has worked as a carpenter, painter, tour guide, and truck driver. His stories have been published in *Story*, *The Graywolf Annual Four*, *Ploughshares*, *Bomb*, *Glimmer Train*, *Zoetrope*, and *Playboy*. He lives with his family in Kentucky, where he is an assistant professor of English at the University of Louisville.

ABOUT THE TYPE

This book was set in Sabon, a typeface designed by the well-known German typographer Jan Tschichold (1902–1974). Sabon's design is based upon the original letter forms of Claude Garamond and was created specifically to be used for three sources: foundry type for hand composition, Linotype, and Monotype. Tschichold named his typeface for the famous Frankfurt typefounder Jacques Sabon, who died in 1580.